Fables, Fairy Stories, Folk Lore and Fantasies

by

Tom Sheehan

Cyberwit.net
HIG 45 Kaushambi Kunj, Kalindipuram
Allahabad - 211011 (U.P.) India
http://www.cyberwit.net
Tel: +(91) 9415091004 +(91) (532) 2552257
E-mail: info@cyberwit.net

Printed at Repro India Limited.

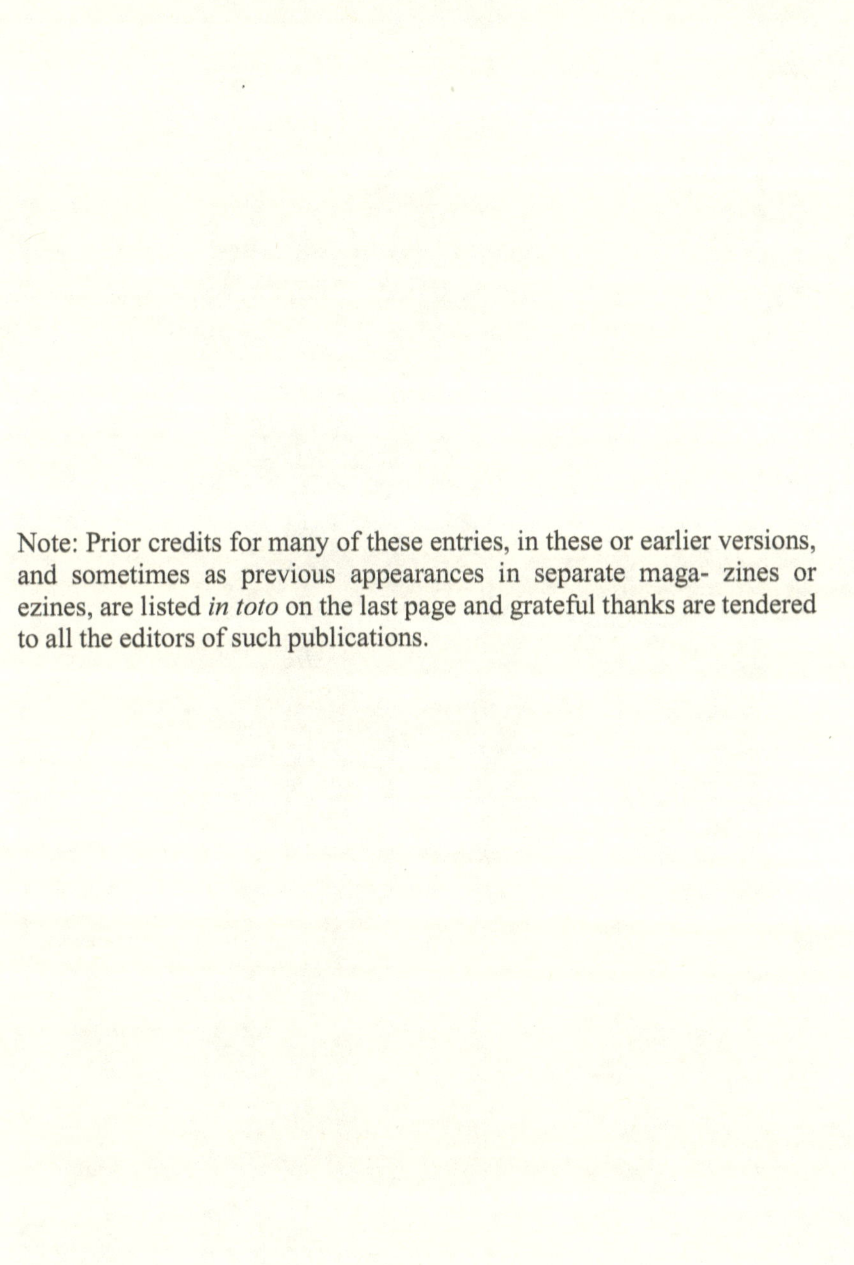

Note: Prior credits for many of these entries, in these or earlier versions, and sometimes as previous appearances in separate maga- zines or ezines, are listed *in toto* on the last page and grateful thanks are tendered to all the editors of such publications.

Boots

At the Last Good Find Saloon, in Tremont, Texas, two old pards, Josh and Max, at the end of a hard day, come in off the trail.

A third man, tall, rugged in the face and across the shoulders, early forties, enters the saloon shortly after them, and walks to the bar. He is wearing a wide sombrero, a dark blue vest over a lighter blue shirt, dark pants and no boots or gun belt. On his feet are strange looking "slippers," to use another term.

Josh, a tall cowpoke and strangely neat as a pin, says to his pal, "Hey, Max, who's the gent in the girlie boots?"

Max, thinking it over, says, "Reminds me of the lady works the post office in Laramie, Suzie something. 'Member how she hid her feet all the time, the silly looking shoes she wore, like they'd fit a whole horse or even two of them."

Both cowpokes laughed at the memory.

Josh, to the stranger, says, "Hey, mister, how'd you come by those things you got on your feet? Don't you wear a real man's boots like all us others do? Good cowboy boots for wearing working spurs, riding horse, herding cattle? I'd allow you can't put no spurs on them things.'" He shook his head in anticipation of a silly answer.

The stranger, nodding, breaks into a wide grin, looks down at his feet for the longest spell, which seems to unnerve Josh, and replies, "These things on my feet are my squeakers, as I call them. They make funny sounds when I walk while my real boots are getting fixed by the harness maker down the street. Other than that, my feet are all my own concern, son. And so is what I wear on my feet, on or off a horse."

Josh, suddenly thinking he's been put down, says, "You poking fun at me, Mister? I don't think I like that. What if I was to whip those silly looking things off your feet, them squeakers?"

The stranger, not yet agitated, quietly replies, "Well, son, I expect you'd find one hand broken or one wrist, your tongue hanging out of your mouth more tired than it is right now, and me climbing all over you just for the hell of it. How's that for a sissy-footed cowpoke just looking to please his throat?"

Josh, threatened, finding his own composure working up, stands and says, "Hell, mister, I don't like your tone none and you ain't even wearing a gun."

"That's the whole point of it, son," the stranger says, "I ain't wearing a gun, so you can't use yours on me if you had that faulty thought come to your mind, which I observe is busier than it ought to be instead of enjoying your whiskey like you ought, never knowing when you might get the taste of the next one. You'd find yourself in the jail for at least one night and maybe more if you were to pull the trigger on an unarmed man."

Max, suddenly seeing what might be coming, cautions his pal. "Josh, better let it go now. Now ain't the time to get this man all riled up. He ain't done nothin' to you."

Josh, still upset, says, "I just don't like his looks, how he talks, how he dresses. He don't look like no cowboy to me."

The barkeep, having heard the whole dialogue, begins to tap the bar top like he's marking time. Finally he says, "Son, pay attention to your pard here, and to the gent you're antagonizin'. It just ain't in your best interest to rile him up and get my place messed up over a pair of funny looking feet critters. And he's a whole lot of right by saying he'll be all over you in good fashion before you can blow your nose or draw on your weapon."

Josh, really agitated, replies, "You think I ain't fast enough to draw and get a bead on him?"

Before Josh can move, the stranger slams a fist in his face, pulls Josh's gun from his holster and trains it on Max.

The stranger says to Max, "Pick him up real easy, son, and take him outside and dump him in the water trough. Tell him, when he's fully awake, sober as he'll ever be, he can get his gun down at the jail. I'm finishing off my drink now and going back to work. Before I get there, you better get your friend put in one of those cells and make sure the door is locked and the keys hung proper. He's going to be madder than hell later tonight. You must know that, you being his pard."

The stranger walks out of the saloon, the squeakers on his feet making a distinctive noise as he leaves the room. The door closes with another squeak.

Max says, as he's trying to pick up his pal, "Barkeep, who the hell is that guy? What's his name? What's he do around this here town?"

Barkeep, holding back the easiest smile, has all the answers. "That's Jed Hollander. He's the head of the Texas Rangers. He's one of the real good lawmen in the whole territory. Probably the damnedest best one of all. Tell your pard he don't want him on the other side of anything. And if I was you I'd make sure I get that hothead in jail pronto lest he starts to agitatin' the law. Won't pay him to do so."

Max, shaking his head, having felt something like this coming his way, says, "Is that man that good? As good as you say?"

The barkeep, glad there's been no fight, gives his answer. " For ten, twelve years he's been between whatever's bad and whatever's good in all this territory, all the way up as far as Plimpton, and you gotta cross the ferry there to get away from him."

Max, hustling his friend erect, who's shaking his head, wobbly, like he's been hit by a mule's kick. "Is he a married man, this Hollander gent, this Ranger?"

The barkeep, waving his hands like a flagman on the railroad, says, "Whoa, there, son. Why do you ask such a question? You sure don't want to go in that direction. Not if your life was to depend on it. That ain't likely safe from any angle no matter how the hellos go 'twixt who and whoever."

Max, smiling sheepishly, gives his answer. "Not me, mister. I'm no lover boy, but Josh here thinks he's the whole shebang to any woman he fancies, and don't miss much that way either. It's like his getting-even weapon, if you know what I mean. Seems as though he's been raisin' that kind of hell since he was halfway to the saddle, maybe even 'afore he saw all the sights the barn was holdin' on to. And in the time I been around, that's all the way to Houston and half the ranches in between. Second thought, probably three quarters of 'em. He's like fire and ice, that boy, the miracle worker's what he is. Heats 'em up and leaves 'em cold and him on the trail again. I wouldn't want to count how many times he's been chased down the trail and the guns goin' off behind him and him laughing like a damned fool, but smilin' like the ears on his head was really red and black and pointin' the way to hell itself."

"He leave any kids on the way?" the barkeep wonders aloud.

Max, still holding Josh erect, says, "I'd guess half the kids in this part of Texas have that same long clean nose and those deep blue eyes like the whole ocean was here sayin' hello to one girl at a time. He just gets meaner'n hell if I tell him about them husbands lookin' half the world over for him." He laughed loudly, and continued, "And their women, too."

"Why's he like that?" the bartender asked. "He's a decent lookin' boy."

Max, thinks it over and says, "My guess he hates what he can't be. He knows he ain't ever goin' to be a good husband or father or plain law-abidin' son of the west. It just ain't in him for such goodness."

Barkeep: "And you? Why are you like this?"

Max: "I can't be what I want to be either. Simple as that. And that Ranger scares me to Kingdom Come as I should know better."

Barkeep: "I'm bettin' he ain't done his bit yet, son. He don't like bad guys, and 'specially those that play women for trinkets and husbands for fools. The law and most men say women this side of the saloon ain't fair game for any drover comes off the trail like he's the angel itself but ain't.

Josh is taken by Max from the saloon.

The scene shifts to the jail where Josh is in a cell. A woman, young, attractive, the Ranger's wife, Alma Hollander, enters at noontime carrying a tray of food.

Alma: "I have your lunch here. Please step back and I will place it on the floor. I'm Mrs. Hollander."

Josh: "I know who you are, sweet one. You're the girl who escaped from that bright moon I was studying all last night after I got locked up in here, the one the moon didn't want to let go of, afraid you'd get scooped up by some lovesick cowboy like me who thinks Texas women are the most beautiful women in the whole world, especially the married ones. Your husband is a real nice fellow, if he is what he seems to be with someone like you at hand. He does have a great eye for beautiful ladies. How I wish I was not in here, lost to the world, lost to the fairest ladies in the world."

Alma (turning to exit after placing the tray on the floor): "Just eat your meal, Josh. That's all you have to do. You'll have your chance someday at true love."

Josh: "I just wish it could be you, Ma'am. No moss growing all over me. When I move on, there'll be some live wishing going on here. You'll just be in the mix then, like a dream that never happened, a beautiful woman locked into a lonely town where the moon can die every night, like death comes on every breath of time if you let it."

Alma: "You are a smooth one, Josh."

Josh: "Knowing my name for starters is all it takes. Now let me dream how it might be. I'll let you know how it goes some other time when I'm shuck of here."

Alma is about to leave and Josh snakes his hand through the bars and grabs her by the hair. Immediately, he covers her mouth with his other hand and pulls her against the bars of the cell.

Josh: "That prairie rat of a husband of yours shouldn't let high and mighty you work like a slave. You got some comeuppance coming to you, you and that man of yours thinks he's the world to you. Well, soft lady, you got some news coming your way."

Josh shifts his position to get a better grab on her, and Hollander steps into the cell room.

Hollander: You keep your hands on her and you're dead before you hit the floor.

Josh: "I got the knife here, high and mighty one, and I'll cut her pretty face so you won't want to look at it come morning any more. I'll mark her fearsome, Ranger boy, real fearsome."

Hollander: "She'll probably do what Chico does when she yells at him."

Alma, a quizzical look on her face, thinks, sees her pet dog being corrected, smiles, and then ducks, as Hollander fires one round high onto Josh's shoulder. It knocks him across the cell. Alma falls free of his grip, the dull knife from the food tray falls to the floor harmlessly.

Hollander: "You're going down into the third level at the penitentiary. You won't see the sun for a few years if you can stand it. I'm willing to wager you'll be nearer to Hell than you are right now."

Location is occasionally a state of mind.

High Rise Rental

From the west the late afternoon sun was resplendent on the grass, reflections shimmering in waves, comfort oozing in the land. Scruffy the Squirrel, basking for the 8th day in a row, watched some of his pals still scurrying about, harvesting, hauling, and lifting construction material into treetops for the coming winter.

He sat back to watch the energy at work, and let it be, let it go on, let it be done. Time, at the moment, was for enjoyment. He napped on top of his fat tail.

So, the days took turns at rote and repetition, one being the other, nothing amiss between the two.

Now and then he'd wake and think about Old Crow's Realty in the far corner of the yard; as ever, they had a lock on the market. That'd be the answer to his housing problem, if there was one, when the time came.

Sleep took him easily again.

When the chills came, seemingly of a sudden twist in the landscape, or was it a twist of time, he knew he'd have to hurry before getting shut out of a good rental. Rushing about, hurry at him for the first time in the failing year; he headed to Old Crow's Realty.

"What have you got for rentals now, Old Crow?" he said."

"Prime as usual, Scruffy. Prime as usual. You know we've been located in the area for years, almost 20 now, and have had an enviable reputation all that time. When I tell you I have a high-class high-rise rental, last one on the market, you have to realize I am not pushing it. Super construction. Tight as the proverbial drum. Built for the comfort of a renter as particular as yourself, provided you get yourself into this deal. In fact, business is so good, me and the little swinging winger will be in Florida, at the condo, and running the used car agency, before you can flap your tail."

"You've done that good this year, Old Crow?"

"Have I ever!" Old Crow let out a cawing cry that could be heard clear across the pond.

"What's the deal?" Scruffy said, resting back on the grass.

"Cash on the drumhead, Scruffy. You drive a hard bargain."

"I'll take it," said Scruffy, leaping up as he saw a few other squirrels edging their way. "Here's my money. Where is it, this high-rental?"

Old Crow, cawing to his better half, grabbed his little bag and pointed to the farthest maple tree in the most distant part of the yard. "Near the top. Next to the last branch up. It's out on the far reach of the limb, with a great view."

Slowly, feeling the gratitude swelling in him, and a sense of good luck, Scruffy climbed the tree as directed by Old Crow, whose wings could be heard in take-off, and found himself at the door of a bee hive hanging from the branch, with a door he could not fit through.

Seeing is believing, or trial is better than terror.

How It Must Have Gone, Making Character

December gave us both a gray day, thick as hardpan, sitting-down thick, a neutral sadness running pole to pole, a day that cried for work or laughter. Work wins out, I told son James, barely three and barely to my thigh. I dressed him for the full adventure; gloves soft as strung rabbit's neck, stocking cap puffed out of lamb, jacket thick with duck's outside, a twist of blue knot sitting under chin, two-ply boots denser than a truck tire.

Jamie leaned penguin-like, lumpy, starchy tight, not quite sure of feet or balance point, where the fulcrum of his day angled, or what could tip him this way or that.

I sat him, nugget of a boy, deep in the van among chainsaw, rip ax, six-pound maul, and the pair of blunt wedges I had worn feverishly down through full reams of trees.

Oh, James likes iron, how it calls attention to itself; hidden core ringing at his feet, the hard touch remembered on cold days, surfaces demanding the sweat of hands.

He likes iron forcing its way in or through, iron beating on or back in brittle echoes, that sprouts handles and odd points and sharp edges; iron changing shapes of shapes, moving together or ever apart, iron crying for the sweet will of muscle.

James comes bound to move earth, to carve pieces to his wanting, his need. He comes magnetic. Tools move to him, are drawn by his hands, heart's thirst, shoulder coming poised behind the ingot, with the shaking that little boys give off. Some monger's fire simmers in his eyes; his lungs have bellow burst, puff of dream. A dynamo hums in him, sings, trembles down the limbs he brings to tasks, a flywheel set in motion, *gearage* grab. He clanged and banged and rang aloud in the back of the van, echoing himself among harsh tools, rang hard as them, wavered as a tuning fork today's wand, gave me in the driver's seat fair music of the shop, beat of the forge at fire, early shape of man in the ringing light of coming on to size, pig iron breakout from the harvest of heat, furnace essence, the brazier soul coming through a sense of fire, son where the welding works.

Oh, we bend here in a parade of tasks, endless marching to orders we are born ever to obey, the expense of our energies. Each of us must light his own ample fire, as James must light his. Failure is here, not burning off the energy, not using up the waiting ghost that resides within.

Now James, my son, comes beside me moving up in time, rattling with tools he will spend his life with or always at, the promise of something Excalibured, the deeply driven, driven out or drawn. The hunger swell that swells some souls must swell in him. At length he will move the mountain in the way, will bend keen tool edge on the steepest edge of Earth as he moves Arthurian in his life. But then, we came at last to dream and destination; a wide field, a thick butt of maple tree, monarch dropped along the avenue, once the carrier of a hundred fallen nests, donned a thousand rains, worst of storms, wore scars of lightning zippered on its bark.

Into this field was brought tree's death. And we come, James and I, to scavenge, to pick as ants, gulls or high vultures what is left of the dying or the dead; a father and son looting what is left of the maple's being, faint yellow core.

A pair of deed-takers, two men of tools, making hard music of twin cutters as I whipped my saw into quick frenzy. It loves good wood, slab of thick hides, the inner rings hundreds high and counting.

James held his ground, the maul too heavy to lift but handle operable as rudder stick, able to steer the day to someplace on. His eyes measured all three-feet down into the butt the saw's cut would hasten, blinked at the majestic toss of sawdust and chips hosing out beneath rapid chain, figuring what it takes to earn the saw, how much tool it was, what its sound meant in a field where our maple died some more.

Trees and tools have made the man the world over (except at the ice caps as we know them.)

The Simple Monster

The Simple Monster can cure blindness, bent legs, curved spines, hiccups, curled toenails, but his bite is lethal. He is magic, but he can hurt. He sits at the end of alleys, in dark recesses, in old doorways where doors don't open at the first push, and in corners of houses you used to visit but all the people there have died or moved away and your parents dare not enter such premises fearing all the disease left behind in that place after death is catchy.

Oh, you've seen him even if you won't admit it, there at the edge of the lawn on a half-moon night when shadows dance without music, like a willow-the-wisp. Or he's at the end of the hallway down from your bedroom door where the darkness crawls into itself and plays more games than you can imagine. Do you remember the unheard sound of music left in the corner of a closet, the attic, that dark spot over behind the furnace in the cellar, or behind the barrels in the garage? That is the sound that hums without being heard, sings without words, finds meter without the air knowing it is being moved by nothing that is real in this whole world. He is behind the music that can't be heard.

Think he's real? You can call on him if you have the will.

His name is Goodandnow, but don't let that fool you, because at the end of his suspenseful name comes big surprises that you won't like, like ropes, manacles, handcuffs, buffeting, mace as wild as a September-October wind in the Bahamas, silken knots on the ropes so you won't think your binds are permanent, or screams so close to your heart you could be drowned in their soft echoes. But don't twist too much because you might choke yourself, lose your breath, put your blood into knots too big for the meaningful flow.

He says he is never lonely because all kinds of kids find him when they want to get that little shudder up the backside they don't get elsewhere, but that's because they don't look elsewhere. There's no hesitation in his shudder, that's for sure. He's the real thing when it comes to ghosts or monsters or ultra-beings on the outer edge of everything that seems sane and responsible. There are nights he is suspended by a length of rope dropping down out of the tallest tree in the backyard or in the whole neighborhood, like he is a dummy playing at being dead. But we all know he is not dead yet. Not on your life. He is too scary for solid thought, too, because if you thought about him being what he is, you'd move away or get a new life or find another ghost to feast on, one whose bite isn't as bad, or as horrible.

But once in a blue moon, he comes out of the cemetery on a cold night carrying all the pumpkins that have been left on gravesites of grandmothers and grandfathers who told scary stories to all their grandchildren just about every night while they were growing up, but never once after they joined the Boy Scouts, or played on a team with other boys or girls, or dated a friend from school. And he strews the streets with pumpkin seeds after cars and trucks have rammed all the pumpkins to waste. He does that because he is mean and never lets a vengeful thought escape him or go off without being used, employed, set free to do his bidding, to frighten you, to break your sense of connection to something real and warm and in the best part of yourself.

Once, when he got into a horrible fight with another superhuman being, in the jumble of arms and legs and the knots that wrestling bodies bring about by great accident, he bit down viciously on the leg curved across the front of his mouth.

Guess what?

He bit himself so savagely that he bled to death.

Transparency

The stories have made the local rounds for years by tradesman who often gather at the end of their work week to soften a harsh throat, meet up with old friends, tell of restitutions made on the spot, in a moment of discovery or illumination. I like to think I've heard them all during my short tenures as laborer, carpenter, working on open steel, but I know I haven't. Some of them may be common knowledge, but many are enjoyable. A few are favorites and I like to hear "eyewitnesses" tell them again, like the ready-mix concrete truck driver who dropped a half-yard of excess load into the convertible of his wife's boyfriend, parked too auspiciously outside his home. Or the fence man, knowing he would not get paid by his ex-brother-in-law, erected a new fence six inches onto the neighbor's property and sat back and watched judgment come to hand.

But my favorite is the brick mason who was hired by a contractor to put up a fireplace and chimney addition to a house the contractor was fully restoring. The contractor had a poor reputation of paying for work in any timely fashion, often delaying payment for months at a time, such as just short of court and sundry expenses.

The restoration site was near the home of a friend who knew both individuals, and he sat back to watch the "long proceedings."

The job was finished, the rehabbed house placed on the market, and one chilly day soon after, with a potential customer checking out the site, my friend saw smoke pouring out the windows of the house and the front door, all which had been quickly opened.

The commotion started.

The contractor called the brickie who was shortly on the scene.

The contractor said, "I'm embarrassed in front of a potential buyer. I lit a fire to show him how good the fire could be on a cold day, and the chimney doesn't work. Smoke poured out into the room and drove us out of the house. You didn't do a good job."

"You didn't pay me," the brickie said. "Pay me and I'll fix it."

The contractor paid the brickie, who went up on the roof with a brick, dropped it down the chimney, breaking the pane of glass he had set into the chimney, just in case.

At times, more than glass is transparent.

Also Henry

Jim Hedgerow was the boss of Riverbank Cemetery's burial crew, and this morning he was scratching to make sure he had enough help to "open up" a few places for "quick deposit."

"Monday," he said to his gang, "is a pain. You all know that. We've got two late shows to open up and I have heard whispers there'll be a third. So, we have our work cut out for us today."

He looked casually at his number one man, Bill Blakeslee, and said, "Bill, take a peek in those trees down at the end of the river road. I've heard some rumbles about night-time shenanigans going on down there. Fellows sleeping out there will be gone come the cold weather. I know they fold up and hide their few blankets and an old shelter-half once in a while so we won't find them. They've done that all summer. Hell, I know there's a few old vets in that group, and I won't chase them out on a bet, even if the Police Chief or the Board of Selectmen tell me to do so. We owe them."

He sent off a slow salute to the far end of the cemetery. His crew understood the acknowledgement.

The following morning, Blakeslee said, "Jim, some of that ground near those first two we dug yesterday seems like something's been in there. Maybe an animal. A big one. Dirt is scattered from under the green tarps we use to hide it during the final services, but I can't figure it out."

Hedgerow said, "Will the cement vaults fit down in there okay? That's all I worry about after the hole is dug, of course."

"Oh, yeah, that looks fine. I was just curious, that's all."

The burials went off that week as smooth as ever, and all "insertions" skidded like grease. Hedgerow was pleased at his crew and their dedicated efforts. He told them, at day's end, "If you guys aren't in a hurry to get home, I'll treat everybody to a few pints down at Spud's place. A quick stop. A quick thank you, so there'll be no noise at home."

Six days later, all the sites were fitted with memorial stones containing appropriate inscriptions, grass seed put down on the exposed earth, and the initial watering completed.

In the morning, Blakeslee, at the completion of his morning stroll to make sure all things were okay and still in order, called Hedgerow to one of the new sites. He pointed to a newly inscribed stone that said, "Herbert Sendall 1932-2010" and the next line, "Sarah Sendall 1936 – "

On the stone was also inscribed, with a dull drill of some sort and inlaid with a black paint, the words, "Also Henry."

"What the hell do you think that means, Jim?" Blakeslee said.

Hedgerow mused a bit, nodded, and said, "Probably kids. It'll go away, unless the relatives make a stink about it. Might cost them for a clean-up. Let it rest."

A few days later Hedgerow was in the diner down the street. One of the homeless vets he knew spent some of his nights in the trees by the cemetery, and worked as a dishwasher in the diner, was talking at the kitchen door to someone outside. "Yeh, a few nights ago, we had a service and had to put old Henry down. But he's safe now. Out of all the hullabaloo."

Hedgerow saw him toss off a quick salute.

In some cases, eternity may not be forever.

Carpenter Ants in the Squirrel House

The carpenter ants at the union hall, read the posters on the opportunity board and massed for the task. George the Squirrel had asked for a contractor's team to do some steep remodeling work as half his tree home had been bruised seriously by hurricane winds.

George was ecstatic when he saw the army of ants arriving for work, the long file of them making him think of elite infantry on the march or an army of red caps descending on the Silver Streak when it came into the train station from clear across the country, baggage galore in the mix. He was stunned by the sight; precision, energy, promise unveiled just for him.

The ant energy, amassed and exhibited in front of him, made him feel good, like he was a judge at an award ceremony, or a general at a field parade. A special sense of appreciation found root in him and he thought quickly of a feast of nuts waiting for him under the grass, waiting to be dug up and enjoyed.

He was beside himself. The memory of the fierce wind was blown away by his own pleasure. George, to appease that hunger, went hunting in the very green grass.

After his artful search, his sense of smell coming off as unique, he rested a bit before he decided to come home and check out the job.

The second half of his tree house was gone, chewed up by the long and sinuous line of carpenter ants that had gobbled everything in sight.

"What happened to my house? Where is it?" George said to the ant's boss.

"It's what we promised in the contract," the ant boss said, "to reduce everything to its proper state. That, to us, was total ruin, not partial ruin.

That's what we did. Chewed every stick to oblivion, as only we can do. Even better than the beavers over there on the pond."

He waved his troops homeward.

Don't be lazy when it comes to reading service contracts.

Dress Codes

They flocked into the huge auction barn like two gaggles of geese, light blue and dark blue in dress and bonnets, the Amish ladies on a Saturday night out in Middleton, Ohio. I understood the light blue dress denoted the maidens in the group, and the dark blue the matrons. The chatter was non-stop, the laughter as well, mostly from the light blue sect, as they grouped by color code in row upon row of folding chairs.

In the distance, lightning set the tone for that far locale, and colored the air about the auction with a sense of excitement and expectation.

I ruminated on the little that I knew about them: that the ladies were excellent house help and the men were carpenters and barn builders extraordinaire, and that they lived according to a strict code. About them was an admirable uniformity, a close likeness of selves, a communion of sorts.

The auctioneer, wearing dark-rimmed glasses, a red bowtie showing a bit of age in the gathered knot, a voice that came from a low diaphragm, egged the crowd into a quick fun festival. If he sat in the midst of the audience, he'd be easily picked as the auctioneer. The magnetism was alive on him.

The first piece of the auction came and went, as did a dozen pieces, each one seeming to stretch the value range. Competition, at the auctioneer's subtle spurring, grew and grasped a good portion of the crowd. And excitement grew with a few pricey competitions.

The giggles and frivolity of a Saturday night out also grew apace. I was marveling at the honest gayety of the Amish ladies.

That's when I saw a light blue maiden, one row in front of me, and one seat over to the left, reach into her deep dress pocket and take out a small jar with a perforated cover on top. She nudged her near companions on both sides, elicited giggles and laughter from each one, and unscrewed the cover on the jar. I saw the motion of soft whiteness emerge from the jar as she placed it down on the floor beside the hem of her flowing dress.

It was a live, white mouse that slipped out of the jar, gained some position knowledge and went on survey.

It took no more than 3-4 minutes for pandemonium to break loose in the major part of the audience, as well as a prim and proper laughter that built to a small thunder of appreciation within the Amish ranks. If they clapped hands, it could not have been louder, or more joyous.

Dress codes often loose character traits that surpass the ordinary.

Game-time Suitcase

It was the mother I first noticed, not the daughter, no more than 3 or 4, at her heels. The suitcase in the woman's hand was not a giant one. It could be carry-on on most airlines, but it was sky blue, looked to be new as a shiny penny, and was heavy. I could tell by her walk, the tilt of her shoulders, the slowing down approach as she came down the foul line from the left field entrance.

No fan ever brought a suitcase to a high school baseball game. I wondered if her son needed an extra drink, required an extra meal, or was shy on his medicine. Her son was the catcher on the team getting their warm-up at infield practice. The ball left his hand and found acceleration as it made the rounds, third to second to first, back to third, to home. The ball sang as it moved, the gloves echoed like shoulder pads on shoulder pads in a football game. The ball flew faster.

The daughter waved to her big brother, not quite oblivious to her, not daring to ignore her with Mom on hand. Cagily, he waved back to her. She responded. I figured, right then, there had to be at least a dozen years between their births.

Big brothers, I knew, were special. So were kid sisters.

Infield warm-up continued, then the coach banged fly balls to the outfielders with a fungo bat; all was normal at the start of a game. The kid sister continued on behind the backstop, again waving secretly to her big brother, who waved back, but more openly this time.

They sat on the first row of the bleachers, behind the backstop, protected from foul balls, wild throws, and incidents.

This first time was the revelation; I stared at the suitcase. What does one carry to a high school baseball game in a suitcase, a blue-ish purple one, a heavy one? I guessed it was not Ken and Barbie at ease, waiting for the hands of the little girl, waiting for miniature romance, small dividends, and little excitements.

The umpire behind the plate, in deep and thick blue accessories, yelled out, "Play ball." The girl's brother, the home team catcher, put his cap on backwards, dropped the mask over his face, pounded his glove, looked at his pitcher standing at the mound, his left toe on the plate, the ball hidden in his glove as his grip found its target.

Before the first pitch was thrown, the mother, at insistence of her daughter, laid the suitcase on the ground, opened the cover and flipped it wide open. I saw, in one look, a quick look, in miniature, two '55 Mustangs, a '57 Chevy, a Pierce-Arrow so old I could only recognize the headlights on the fenders, a '43 Jeep far removed from its campaigns, a long-gone Desoto, a mysterious Packard with a hood as long as the Erie Canal, and a '54 Pontiac that could have come from my brother's garage.

All of them, in this choice collection, sat atop the first mobile sandbox I had ever seen. Soon, before the first fly ball settled into the left fielder's glove, there were two roadways traced in the sand, a bridge spanned the deep pocket of the suitcase and its offhand cover, and the supply of sand, as if in global expansion, dispersed onto the two continents of the blue-ish purple suitcase.

The little girl, if you must know, missed a homer by her brother in the third inning, a minor skirmish at home plate when a runner tried to knock him over as the throw came into his glove in the fifth frame, and the winning run come home as her brother slid into second base ahead of a long throw, with the crowd noisy as ever.

Preparation, one can imagine, is the name of the game.

Late Bloomers

Evolution begins with origination, initiation, brainstorm, hunch, self-starter mode, or a plain accident, all which may treat the beginning of an idea, a product, or a belief. Like friend Joe or Fred might say, "I thought of it first. It's my invention. The rights should belong to me."

Those stories have been heard for years upon decades upon centuries.

As with ranks and echelon levels in aristocracy and the military and in politics, as well as names of books, stories, poems, one never knows truly what's behind a title, what sets it off, what it entails.

So, it was with our late bloomers, slowly out of the gate, slow to change, slow to adapt, but once up to speed raced headlong into newness. They began a host of changes that paced and raced with new rights, new appreciations, new designs, new methods of exposure, applications that opened eyes far and wide, and leaped into attention in magazine and newspaper advertisements, within show reviews and musicals, upon modular runways that spread perpendicularly into large audiences, and gauged the mansions of some free-thinkers, as we followed chemise, crinoline, drawers, underpants, panties, scanties, step-ins, briefs, bikini bottoms, and the disappearing thong.

As said, one never knows what's behind a name, brand or title.

Mrs. Private Detective

The letter came on a Saturday morning delivery and lay unopened for two days of rushing around, special errands, preparation for a graduation, a grandson's varsity football game, a dance at the club.

Hillary Gooden, a stylish 70 according to her husband Harry, finally managed to settle down, to "tend to bills" and other matters, and opened the letter. She thought it strange that an envelope originating in the same town, was practically block printed, a sophomoric attempt to disguise a familiar hand. She was not suspicious, but she believed in intuition.

The letter, in the same block-type printing, said, "I don't know where you were, but it was Harry's car leaving the inn at Crescent Blvd and Mercy Road. He went out twice during the early part of the night, once to a liquor store and once to a pizza parlor, both in the other end of town. I saw him make the purchases through the windows of the stores each time. He paid cash, did not use a credit card, entered and left each establishment with his hat down over his eyes. It really bothered me, Hillary, and I just had to send this on to you. I'll provide as much detail as I can so you can undertake any due action.

The letter closed with, "A friend."

Hillary's husband Harry said to the Private Detective lady, who they knew lived a short way down the street, "Hillary sent this back to you because you forgot to sign it."

She blanched and blushed and stammered, and said no more, for Hillary had added the following to the bottom of the letter: "If you go to the Devonshire Inn, Room B on the first floor, and look at the back of the bottom drawer of the antique dresser, you will find two inscriptions, HG &HG 5/1/60 and HG & HG 5/1/10. Harry took me there on the one day of our honeymoon and surprised me with another one-night stand for our 50th anniversary. You should have been there, both times. They were special. Don't try to take them from me. HG."

The longest nose often gets bitten off.

The Last in the Race Winner

They had gathered in a sequestered section of grass, the flock of Canadian Geese, in East Boston's Suffolk Downs Race Track. The very early morning hours were spent, as usual, picking up lost coins or currency the track patrons had lost in excitement, deep sadness, or plain misery at losing another bet. Once in a while one of the more astute geese picked up a lost ticket on a winning horse. They'd make a deal with one of the stable dogs, Mackerel, who'd manage to slip it on to his master – some of the winnings would be shared with the geese, one way or another. Mackerel had the know-how.

North Smitty, this year's elected flock leader, not too excited about horse races in particular, thought about the coin and currency they had piled up in a secret holding place. "We ought to wager it somehow," he said, "and at least get some fun out of it."

"Yuh," said Flo Newfie, "we sure know how much fun it ain't for some of the bettors who lose whole chunks of money." There was a distinct pause and measurement in her voice, as she continued, "Sometimes they lose the whole damned mortgage payment, or enough to pay the rent for a month, or buy groceries. How much fun can that be?" She kept shaking her head and her tail feathers.

Bent River, another fly-by specialist of the flock, said, "Let's get ingenious on this matter. Smitty's right in saying we ought to get some fun out of it." He flapped his wings a few times for timing attention. "Like we say, thinking of heading south for the winter, 'We can't take it with us.'"

The whole flock was in stitches over that comment. Flo Newfie even swung her head around and looked at Bent River with a new look in her eyes.

North Smitty had a gander's look about him as he suddenly said, "I got a great idea. Let's bet the bundle on the loser of the last race of the day. Make amends somehow. We study the program and pick who we think will come in last in the last race of the day. Let's see how smart we are. We knock them enough about being stupid," and he nodded at the crowd starting to gather for the day.

"That's a great idea, Smitty," Flo Newfie said, with a new look at the elected leader for the year. "I'll go snag a program of the day from somewhere in the stables. Be right back." She flew off in a low but direct flight and they saw her land behind the last stable. In a matter of minutes, she returned with the race program for the day.

They argued for over an hour as they studied the program listing for the last race.

"Look here," Teddy Wingman said, "this old crone's never won a race in any of her five tries, Nashua Belle. She sounds like a sure winner for us. Can't even finish some times. What about her?"

"Sounds good to me," Flo Newfie said, as she smiled at North Smitty again. "What do you say, Big Guy?"

"Well," said North Smitty, "if that's the consensus."

That's as far as he got in his stand, when the old timer of the flock, Calgary Eddie said, "Look, I've been here longer than all of you on these visits. There's something I'd like to say about some of the things I've seen over the years."

"Go ahead, CE," North Smitty said, "you got the grass."

"I often wondered why some horses get to stand for hours with ice packed around their legs before the race. Then one day it came on me, like the lamp was lit. That horse had leg pains and couldn't finish without his legs being iced down before the race. I saw it a number of times when regular losers, made to stand in ice before the start of his race, won going away. It was like the pain was all gone."

"How do we track that in this race, CE?" North Smitty said.

"One of them's in this last race. Goes by the name of Pioneer Joe. The time he was in ice, he ran away with it. Lost all his other races. In fact, came in dead last in four races, but won the last time out. That's going to change the betting, I'm sure."

"Be right back," Flo Newfie said, and she flew off towards the stables.

In minutes she was back. "Pioneer Joe is not standing in ice now. He looks like a sure loser."

The flock pooled their findings, got it to Mackerel, who managed the bet through his master who understood dog talk.

Pioneer Joe came in dead last, almost dead in his tracks, like the next race was going to be a certain thing.

Sometimes a sure thing is a loser.

The Rabbit versus Turtle Bit

It's happened more than once we know, and this latest race was supposed to end like the others. The rabbit this edition was old Peter Cottontail, and at his advanced age was still faster than the young turtle, Yacky, always mouthing off at the corner of the block. *The Rabbitville News* continued to say, "Experience and speed usually mean first place in many races."

"I can beat that old rabbit two ways to Sunday and then some," young Yacky was saying to the corner denizens after their supper hour. "He's so slow these days he doesn't get home until all hours of the night. Talk about doddering, he misses dinner half the time. Last I heard he's still late for last Thursday's supper."

"Why not race him, Yacky, like the old days, but turn the tables on him again. Give him some good betting odds, or run backwards or go in the opposite direction. Make it interesting. He'll sure bite for it. They all do."

"Who's 'they?'" Yacky said.

"Oh, all them fast trackers. You know the kind, high speeders, rail riders, always leaving us turtles in the dust, like they got a mean streak in them."

"Rabbits with a mean streak? Come on. Get real."

"Well, how come they always want to race us turtles? Don't you think that's mean?"

"Okay, I'll do it," Yacky said, "but instead of the usual stuff, I'll run in the opposite direction on the one-way circle around the block and still beat the tail off him thinking he can rest any time he wants. Those rabbits never change."

Old Peter Cottontail accepted the challenge and the conditions, inner laughter rocking through his frame as he walked off at the starting line. "I have a month of Sundays to do my thing," he said to himself, following the arrows.

Halfway around the run, he realized had not encountered Yacky.

Along with his aged body, his eyes had done tricks on him and he never noticed the direction signs had been altered, and he was far afield of the course.

On a one-way street there's ups and downs, and ins and outs, and there's still more than one-way home.

The Sawyer and the Lawyer, a Fable

The lawyer came out of his house after a noisy storm and hearing the wind blowing all night. He noticed for the first time the way a huge tree was leaning. With another storm forecast by the weather experts, he was afraid that the tree would fall on his house.

He looked in the Yellow Pages for a Tree Surgeon, Woodcutter or Tree Removal Specialist and called a sawyer living on the other side of town.

The sawyer, ready for work, came with his truck loaded with tools, and saw how the tree leaned one way, but was top-loaded with its full growth of summer leaves.

The lawyer said, "Can you chop this tree down so it will fall onto the driveway or the front lawn and not fall on my house?"

Looking up at the tree, the sawyer said," I can drop the tree so that it will not fall on your house, but will fall beside it, between the house and the garage, and not onto the driveway or the front lawn."

The lawyer looked again at how the tree was leaning and said, "I insist that you drop it on the driveway, away from the house. It will be easier for you to carry off the remains. That too is easy to see."

The sawyer shook his head, and replied, "That is not the easy way, the way you want it. It is too dangerous. The tree is over-balanced on one side and will fall that way."

"My good man," the lawyer said, "I can see the tree is leaning this way," and he pointed toward his house. "I do not want it to fall on my house. I will write out and sign a contract that you will cut the tree the way I propose. Will that be sufficient protection for you, absolving you of any blame? And I will prepay you the amount we agree on, all stated in the contract."

The lawyer felt like he was in court again, in control.

"Yes," the sawyer finally said, at length bothered by the lawyer's stubbornness. "I will drop it as you direct, with no question as to the outcome."

The lawyer, with great speed and to stay ahead of the forthcoming storm, drew up and signed the contract, and gave a copy to the sawyer along with the prescribed payment.

The lawyer pointed at the side of the tree trunk where it leaned and said, "Make your first cut here, away from the house, and then cut it from the other side."

The sawyer said, "As you say, sir." He cut a V into the trunk with his chain saw, pulled out the wedge he had cut, and began to saw the trunk from the other side of the V cut. It went swiftly, the second cut, and the tree fell on top of the lawyer's house.

Sometimes a different venue is too far afield even for sworn experts, or pride comes before the fall.

The Ugly Frog and the Bigmouth Bass

The trout was a brilliant rainbow, colors of a memorable arc on his underside, and yet, for all his wariness and guile, found he was hooked at the side of his jaw. I was proud of my catch as I looked down upon him, happy as I could be, until he looked me in the eye and said, "Let me go, Sir. Put me back in, where I belong, and I'll tell you about the frog and the bigmouth bass. It's the biggest story to come out of the pond in years. It's a whopper."

Stunned I was, knocked back on my heels, but I couldn't tell anybody because they'd brand me as a liar, a bigmouth in my own right, a romancer in words.

I said to him, nameless as he'd be, "How do I know you'll keep your promise?"

"I say the same thing, Sir; how can I trust you? If I tell you, you could keep me here, topside, a dry lander, a sucker for a slinky worm. And by the way, was that worm a stale worm? It had an old taste to it. Too long on the shelf, in the cooler, or in your bait box from your last trip? And by the way again, how long has it been since you fished here last, from this same place? There's something familiar about all this. Your look, your tone of voice, and the words you use. Have you noticed?"

"Maybe it was just an old worm," I said.

"Well, I hope you use fresher bait the next time," he said. Like there'll be a next time, I bet he was really saying.

I knew he was using delay tactics. And promising me a great story almost in the same breath. Hah, the nerve of him.

"I just ought to fillet you, dip you in egg yellow and corn meal, and cook you up on a camp stove," I threatened in my deepest voice, "trying to bribe me with the promise of a story, a whopper about the ugly frog and the big mouth bass.”

“Just as I thought,” the trout said, as he rolled over and flipped himself back into the pond, his last words being, “Writers never know where their next story is coming from, or the next review.” The last part sounded like a threat.

It can be said, one never knows who reads his last words or who remembers them.

A White Lie Black as Hell

My Dodge window van, 1975 model, was loaded with family, relatives, and a native guide to fishing holes near Lakeville, New Brunswick. Vacation was exotic, sweeping, new as dawn. I was bent on fishing after driving here and there for seven days, and was guaranteed a day to contemplate beside a stream, a pool of promise, the phantom trout awaiting.

I should have been worn out with pleasure. The night before, in Woodstock's Community Center, we had heard 22 fiddlers, some having driven 100 miles for the get-together, play along with a single violin and a piano for more than two solid hours, folks of the 200 plus audience dancing in the aisles at times. I was spellbound, but felt I needed contemplation beside an idyllic stream. Fishing was my great relaxation.

I drove, at direction of the guide, a relative, for more than three hours, visiting fishing sites, sweet locations, yet feeling that I could not abandon the drive to please myself; we were seeing the inside of Canada.

Impelled, we kept moving, and I was charting a map in my mind for the future.

"One last place I'll show you," the guide said, smiling, knowing my mind and taste I fully believed.

We passed by more potato fields, past more stone walls, sudden tree lines, small copses of trees, then hit a thicker forest for a torturous few miles on a trail that I'd never find in a hundred years.

In one turn of a tough road, I saw Paradise, Nirvana, a beautiful stream unwinding out of a thicker growth of trees hanging like umbrellas over the lead-in to a clear banking and a pool with glassy water. I was mesmerized.

And then I saw a figure, moving shakily, duck for a moment behind a tree. An old man presented himself as he stepped from behind the tree. He was ancient, but amiable-looking, though his movements were slow, doddering. A thin sweater draped itself on his shoulders on this warm day.

He brought a smile to my face, as did a jumper up-stream behind him, a trout with my name on it, the rainbow colors streaming off its bottom side. Then another. I saw them. I heard them. And the old man, possibly deaf, did not turn to note any action behind him, but looked intently at me and the other invaders.

"Good morning," he said, with a sort of phony smile, and then I saw the handle of his bamboo fly rod standing against the tree he had tried to hide it behind.

"Good morning, sir," I said, in the most gracious manner I could muster while the excitement was still alive in me. "How's the fishing here?"

In a remarkably-told white lie, his face locked into honesty itself, eyes suddenly alive with friendliness, disguise hidden, he replied, "Oh, there's no fish in here."

He was the Old Man of the Mountain, the Old Man of the Stream.

His mouth hung open; I imagined his heart almost stopping for a moment, waiting for my response.

I shifted into first gear, a true fisherman making headway.

Possession, the lawyers say, and old fishermen, is nine-tenths of the law.

The Boy at the Bottom of the Ladder

The boy came down his street and saw a ladder leaning against a house, but he did not see anybody on the ladder or on the roof of the house. He wondered why the ladder was there, so he decided to wait and see what happened. He sat at the foot of the ladder and was biding his time, when a man came down the street and said, "You're not thinking about climbing that ladder, are you, young man?"

"No, sir," the boy said. "I'm just waiting to find out why the ladder is here and nobody's using it. I can't see anybody up there at all."

"Did you ever think the man who set up the ladder might be on the other side of the roof?"

"He should have put the ladder up on that side."

"Maybe he went off to get some tools or supplies to do the work he means to do."

"Then why would he put up a ladder so little kids like me might dare to climb up it and maybe fall off the roof?"

"You have a lot of questions for such a little tyke, haven't you?"

"One less than you," the boy said, counting on his fingers.

Reason is often made up of addition or subtraction

The Cross-eyed Jackal of Sagamore Splits

The mother jackal living in the hills above Sagamore Splits, a summer camping area for people of the city-life, left her newborn to get food. She was gone for two or three hours and came back with a piece of cooked meat she had stolen from a campfire while a camper was shaving at the stream. When she returned to the cave where they lived, she noticed the little one's eyes were crossed and he appeared to have difficulty knowing what he looked at.

"What happened?" she said to her little one. "Why are your eyes crossed like that, as if you cannot decide which way to look for things?"

"When you left here you told me to watch both the front and the back of the cave, to keep alert for anyone preying on the newborn like me."

"But you only had to swing your head back and forth to see in both directions, like this," she said, and swung her head back and forth, her eyes peering at the brightness outside and the darkness toward the back of the cave that ran deeper into the heart of the mountain. "This way is so much easier."

"But you can't see both ways at the same time, like I can, just as you told me to do," the young one protested, and further stated his case by adding, "I can see the yellow flowers waving in the breeze out in the forest in front of the cave, and at the same time I can see the snake with red diamonds on his skin that's sitting back there on a shelf of rock looking as if he's hungry enough to eat both of us."

"But I can't see any snake back there," she said.

"That's because you just came in from the brightness of day and the back of the cave is like midnight."

The mother jackal, feeling that her young one was more adaptable to change than she was, did not pursue a change in tactics, being comfortable in her own way. And she completely disregarded the snake with the red diamonds on his skin, as if word from the young did not count.

When, on the following day, she came back with another stolen meal, off a new camper's fire, the snake was coiled in place where she had left her little one.

"Where is my son?" she said to the snake, unable to see deeper into the dark cave.

"Oh," said the snake, "he is still here but you cannot see him now."

"Then he is in one piece?" she asked.

"Yes," said the snake, for he had swallowed the young one whole.

Sometimes nothing is the way one sees it

The Donkey, the Jackass, the Burro and the Mule

They came together in the middle of the Great Plains, miles of wide fields and with no humans in attendance.

Don the donkey, looking around again, said, "Can we believe there's nobody checking on us? No reins. No leather goods of any sort. No old-fashioned plows. No wagons too heavy to trot with."

Jack the jackass said, "Never mind the formalities, have you got the family trees all laid out the way we decided?"

Don the donkey said, "Well, Mike the mule says it's a snap. Has it all done. It's all plain as day. You'll see for yourself, but we all have to be sure right up front about how we run with this."

Bill the burro, smallest of the gathering, said, "What's the final conclusion? That's all I want to know. Is it evident? Do we trust it all the way? My parents are getting a bit squeamish about this sort of stuff. They never heard of DNA, and I think they've been around forever."

Don the donkey said, "Okay, Mike, it's your show."

Mike the mule, very business-like, sitting on his haunches for the big moment, opened up his document case, and pointed to the bottom line. "As you can see, we're all related. Every last one of us."

"How can that be?" Jack the jackass said, looking quizzically at the assembly.

Seeing is more proof than pudding, no matter what it tastes like.

The First Robin and the Worm

Two worms idled on the spring grass, early sun warming the ground. The first worm, having spent a couple of years underground by his counting, said to a younger worm just popping up to enjoy early spring, "Keep your eyes open for the first robin. He'll be mighty anxious after his long flight from down south." He kept his head up, watching the sky overhead.

The newer worm was idling and stretching in the sun. "Even the robin can't deny what this dawn is like, so what can he be looking for that we have not seen already?" This is what he was said, just as the robin landed and pecked at him.

"Now you know," the older worm said, departing the scene.

Timing and observance are often critical for menus and stately meals.

The Grasshopper and the Eagle

The green grasshopper and the black eagle met at the edge of a great river.

The eagle said, "Do you notice how much bigger my wings are than yours? They must be a thousand times bigger."

The grasshopper, in his manner, said, "Are you counting both wings in that equation? I can only look at one of them at a time. They are so far apart I wonder what can hold them together."

The eagle, grumbling, put in his place by the weakest voice imaginable, said, "What is that you are eating, that little portion?"

"This is my holiday celebration meal. It is all I can handle."

"What celebration is that?'

"Why this is the night before the worst storm of the year. Where will you hide during the storm?"

"I hide from no storm," the eagle said with great pride. "I can ride out any type of weather."

When the storm hit, blinding snow driven by a fierce wind and the temperature plummeting, the grasshopper was deep in a crevice in the warm earth and was saved from the savage storm.

In three days, the grasshopper peeked out from his hiding place and saw the glowing sun and basked in the sweet rays of sunshine. He asked the turtle if he had seen the big eagle, and the turtle said, "The last I saw of him, he was heading south."

Vacations, as one might realize, are sometimes planned on the spot.

The Hawk and the Eagle and the Rabbit

The argument took place in front of the whole forest crowd, the hawk and the eagle exclaiming their talons were the sharpest in the world, the quickest and could hold more in one grasp than any other pair of talons, or the clutch of any animal in the forest.

"It's so easy to prove," each one said in turn.

And perhaps no one was listening to the braggarts.

"Who is to be the judge?" said the big white rabbit, chief of the largest warren in the forest. "The judge must be a leader, be a stick-out with his community viewpoints, and be above all in his character traits, like humility, honesty, perseverance, and all such traits.

"Fat chance we'd find anyone like that here," said the hawk.

"For once in my life, I agree with Mr. Hawk," the eagle said. "We might as well argue at the moon or the morning star."

"Oh, I don't know about all that," said the rabbit. "We have some pretty good stand-up characters right here in our midst. We could find one easily. We must have pride and continuance in our community and not be at a loss in such a predicament.

"Would you volunteer for the task?" the eagle said.

"Of course," the rabbit said, stepping forward, "not a chance that I'd give up on the whole community."

In one swipe of their talons the hawk and the eagle each snatched a good chunk of the rabbit before a breath could be taken by the rabbit and were high overhead and going in different directions.

Boasting, at times, may get you everywhere.

Moment of Truth at the Bus Stop

Every workday morning, two men met at the bus stop in their neighborhood. They had a few moments of morning chatter and then each one began to think ahead to their work day. This ritual went on for months and months until the morning when one man did not show up. The other man, with no one to say hello to, sort of missed his morning contact.

Two weeks passed and the missing man was back at the bus stop, in his usual manner, saying hello to the other man, chatted harmlessly and then stopped talking.

The first man said, "Well, where have you been for two weeks? Did you go on vacation?"

"I was trying to find something to talk about every morning."

"Did you find it?"

"Not yet, but it's coming."

Reticence is often made up of equal parts.

The Whispering

The contest was slated for the barnyard after the lights went out in the farmhouse. All the animals were eligible including the donkey that had been purchased at a local auction by Farmer Jones this very day and was en route to the farm at that very moment

The contest was to determine who of all the animals had the best hearing. It was to be called The Whisper Contest. The Chief Cricket would do the whispering, from a long distance at first, coming by degrees to where the best listener yelled out the correct message. Word went out to all the peepers and frogs to keep quiet while the contest was underway, and the owls, as darkness would be upon them.

The Major Duck of the group, apparently earless but proud of his keen hearing, asked, "Does anybody know anything about this donkey coming here tonight and just in time to be eligible for the contest?" He sounded sour as usual.

"Oh, relax," said Phil the Horse. "His owner died I heard and all his stock was sold off at auction and our boss bought the donkey."

"What's his name? What's his brand?"

"His name's Don the Donkey and he's one of us now. He'll wear our brand, and he's fully eligible to enter the contest, if that's a problem with you."

Just at dusk, truck headlights flashed down the road. Don the Donkey was on his way.

In the truck, knowing his ears were the biggest he'd ever seen, Don folded his big ears flat beside his head so he wouldn't be such a stick-out in the barnyard. He looked strangely different for a donkey.

Don the Donkey was introduced to the others by Phil the Horse. "Somewhere along the line," Phil said, "Don and I might be related." He paused and then said, "Now everybody be quiet and the contest will begin."

In the darkness, the lights out in the farmhouse, the peepers and frogs and owls all at silence, Don the Donkey, feeling comfortable in the blackness, let his ears return to their usual position atop his head, and suddenly blurted out, "What is this strange message that comes to me now?"

"He's the winner," yelled the Chief Assistant Cricket, who knew what the contest message would be.

Personal traits which are often covered up or disguised might be seen as strengths by others.

To the Brim and Back

On April 21, 2004, at the zenith of the sun that somehow fell sideways through the tall windows of his Georgian-style home looking down on the Merrimac River, silence for the moment now an absolute enemy, his mind finding a sudden clarity he had not known in a long time, 71-year old Guillaume *Gee Gee* Poupon threw down his cane and screamed from the head of the stairs, at the world in general and nobody in particular (since there was nobody else in the whole roomy house): *I am tired of leaning. I am tired of being alone. I am tired of this goddamn house holding me like a briefcase. I am out of here.* In a deep Acadian voice, he cursed and the sounds, his own sounds, erupted a smile on his face.

The blood was pumping in his chest, once again being known, cavalier, Vesuvian, *oh that he once had been so young.*

He almost fell down the stairs, but recovered his balance. Life, he had thought for more than a dozen years, had beat the hell out of him. Where the cane landed in the hallway below, he had no idea, only the clattering sound of its now useless strut fading away. He wondered how far he could have thrown the old life with the same gesture. The thought of mere yards did not come to him.

Onto the front porch he went, and there, not twenty yards away, on the edge of the lawn that ran between their two houses, old crony Georges Papilown stared at him. "Yesu Cree, Gee Gee, you been come out of the house now?"

"I'm the new man, Georgy, the new man. I threw away the cane. I'm getting air. Ismelda is long, long enough to get comfortable in her grave. I am out of here." Into the old dialect he fell, as if he were recouping his years, back on the corner with Georgy and the other guys, looking at the night ahead. "I hope the geddam car start. I pray it start." The keys were in his hands. He could not remember what key was the ignition key. "How you say you start dis thing yet, Georgy, eh?"

"Gee Gee, we get that sumnabitch goin' for you, or die tryin'", is swear to you hell and back somehow. Ain't I been sayin' to Elsie that sonbitch gonna rust there, not you but the geddam car, what is it, 1982 Dodge Slanthead? 'Member that night we go Plum Island, find them chickies lookin' at us, we old fishermen then, look at us now. But we coulda raise some hell that night, they lookin' like hell for fun and loose trousers, bet your geddam dollar they wuz loose for the night, and me you fishin' thinkin' like paradise on the geddam hook plain as a worm or a silver trinket for the fishies, how the way brains talk us."

He paused in the middle of an enormous thought. "The tool dies and we go under like it all over. If we get it goin', this geddam car, where the hell you go? Elsie won't let me go with you anymore even to the grave, she says. Go down to the Senior Center. Labertie say it full of hungry women look like they been at nothing but bones for years. Say hello for me, tell 'em Georgy come soon, sooner than we know," and as his voice dropped to a whisper, he added, "She listen like a spy was workin' in her kitchen. Tell me I'm too old to smell the rose never mind the good stuff." He looked behind him, back at his house.

"What she don't know won't get hurt by her. No maybes yet. We could sneak that ride down there, maybe tomorrow, some next day, some next week." He looked around and continued, "Could raise some new hell it could for everybody."

His grin was as secret as the dawn.

Old men know a fierce appetite is a grave danger

From Lubichan by Rail

Oh, believe what you will, sir. I did not ask you to share my place. We leave one place and go to the next. This morning we were in Lubichan, back down the track bed, amid the unbelievable flowers, and cherry blossoms raising havoc with all that's holy in life, and the restraint such blossoms have on the heart, as if all cannot be believed, goodness being what it is. You know what goodness is, beneficence. The snowfall of them is illustrious, memorable, God himself frozen upon air, hanging out with the boughs and blossoms, oh resplendent in replacement each year.

You think it not so, but do not wake this tired one to ask his version, his mind's eye of the sights there; to ask what is the life of the bee as humble as his drone, yet see his architecture, his marvels, close your eyes and remember what he of little wings has done and great fear it might not get done. They are African bees, you know, fiery hearts come with near phantom wings taking up palace in spots where sweetness lingers, waits. Oh, sir, they are leopards at what they do. He knows his bees well, calls them leopards of the air.

Later we will be in Qat me Dere where the onions are and dark grapes sucking beauty out of earth and pouring it back. At the end of the valley, beside a small house, sits a remnant palm yielding a handful of dates each year, fearing also to let go its long grasp. Don't wake him to ask what the fields of Qat me Dere look like, though it is a gift he brings to all places; how fields lay out like a woman her lover looks down upon in the new breath of dawn, how a river at evening collects all the silver coin a day has left hanging for the last legs of its miracle, how a smile takes a mouth from one place to another so bright the moon asks how.

I beg you, do not jostle him, do not jostle him. Ask no questions of him; he tires in his quick pursuit, so far reaching, so rich the details he brings dazzle you. Do not cough again like that, sir. It does not become you, trying trickery. Ruses be off! Let him be. Let him rest. Let his eyes, those glorious orbs, those rooted measurers of beauty and of beast, let them rest, have their short moments of peace, oh recoup their benefaction. Let him be until his call comes; he knows the where and when, and he tells me what scans the horizon and the smallest alley. Even now I know you move in the light or against the light, your shadow moves there, but he tells me what's in the heart of a shadow. He sees what I do not but shares his gift with me. Oh, sir, do not waken him yet.

The blind, it has been said, see deeper than sight.

The Secret of the Maple

It all began as a hum, not deep, not sharp, but a hum. Locker thought it was turnpike traffic at first, the way semis at times gather in huge road collections that sound like storms at sea, rolling over the land to where he stood. He could picture the parade of huge Kenworth and Reo and International rigs pounding down the road. Oftentimes the weather changed the sound, a kick in the wind, a sudden rise or drop in temperature, a horn or nearby generator making its own waves, or a scream at twilight.

On each occasion he found himself in the cemetery, standing among hundreds of grave stones, paying attention, he thought, to all the territory around him. His father was three years here under grass, under the stone, under the tree, which, as a sapling, he had dug out of the earth at the edge of the swamp and planted its roots beside his father's grave. He knew the reach of the roots and it did not disturb him, believing the changes in the corpse started after a year's interment, the embalming lasting only so long before a new kind of life exerted its power down below. If he let it, that new microbic power, it would make him shiver, knock him off his feet, get him closer to the old man who had said, "If you don't hurry after me, listen for me."

He never knew where or when to listen, but assumed the cemetery was the best place to start. Maybe later, at home, or in the cabin up on the lake, Vermont steep as ladders beside him, he'd find instructions saying otherwise, his father's voice in plea, prayer or promise.

The first leaf he picked up carried a scent with it that was not maple, but known to Locker, though he had trouble identifying the original source of the aroma. It was not maple. It was not sugary. It was not tree.

He smelled it, then he studied it, and for some unknown reason that he spent hours and days and weeks trying to reconstruct that initial demand, he placed the leaf against his ear. As faint as dawn, as faint as a light mist on the lake in Vermont when the sun first filters through it, as faint as a hummingbird off the end of the porch in the late sunlight cruising at an angle, he heard the word, a single word but with two syllables, "Ever."

For an hour he listened to the word. "Ever" did not fade, do a fall-away, or disappear from the auditory possibilities of sound. "Ever" it said, a constant though whispered word.

Other leaves began to fall. "No," he said aloud, as if to condemn any thought that was rising in him. "No," he said again, shaking his head, not daring to believe what he dared to believe, hoped for. But he picked up another leaf and went through the same ritual as the first leaf had gone through. He drew a strong breath into his nose. Then held the leaf against one eye so he could study the filaments of the veins that coursed through it, then, as the final resort, the stretch for believability, he placed the second leaf against his ear.

No doubt existed now, for plain as it could be said, "Fortune" came to him, still with the same thinness of voice, the slow and subtle whisper, the word came on his ear.

Another leaf fell, a bright golden-yellow-red leaf wearing some of the sun and carried another word for hearing. He placed the three leaves in his pocket, the third one carrying his name, the way his father called him into the house at darkness when he was a boy.

"George," the leaf said, plain as any measure, any sound, his own name. "George," it had said, in his father's insistent voice, though faint, subtle, whispered.

"George."

George Locker looked around, the nearest tree over 40 yards away, in the next section of the cemetery, but not a maple. He was not sure what kind of a tree it was, but it was not a maple. Then he looked at the ground, as more leaves fell around him. He scurried to grasp them and placed them in his car.

He raced around and around and knew he was losing the game, so he made a desperate decision. Jumping into his car, he drove a half mile to his house, retrieved two rakes from his garage and a large drop cloth, then went back to the cemetery.

He started raking leaves, raking words, raking the book of them, his father's words that fell upon the ground, that rose out of the ground as roots leaped up.

It was just past 8 AM and visitors and cemetery workers were on the scene and watched as George Locker raked up piles of leaves onto the drop cloth and emptied each load into his car. He begged others to help, and soon, with some kind of contagion he had ignited, the visitors and the cemetery workers began to help him. Some even shook the lower limbs of the tree to shake loose the clinging leaves.

From a distant place, an unknown place, the wind gathered a hush and a rush into itself and slapped the tree from top to bottom limb. More leaves fell, more words gathered, more messages were deposited in his car.

There was an exultant joy when the last leaf was cornered from a little whirl of wind, a tiny geyser of wind. A cemetery worker handed that last leaf to George Locker, content to know he would not have to rake any more leaves from this tree as part of the perpetual care of the gravesites.

When he handed the leaf to Locker, Locker placed it against his ear and heard, "Amen."

All winter George Locker wrote the book he heard his father read to him.

Words come on your horizon only when you listen.

The Kelly Green Colt

This story can begin anywhere; back there, up here, at the site of the Double-NN ranch, on the dusty roads beyond the ranch, with any one of the characters caught up by the presence of the colt, by the colt itself that caused the uproar. But I suppose it comes mostly from the itinerant peddler Jervis Bracko who moved predominantly east and west with his wagonload of goods and his special delivery of tales, rumors and the "latest fact of fiction that spurs my mind to these doors."

The Double-NN Ranch of Shaun Treacy was one of Bracko's favorite stops, and in his lexicon soon became *The Dublin Ranch,* a piece of Ireland at long reach.

The day that Bracko had come away from seeing the new colt at The Dublin, he went in haste, his stories suddenly fortified with the most mythical of his tales. It was something the Little People must have weaved for The Dublin, and he himself had seen the physical proof of it all. a stark, green-all-over colt, born to the mare Cavanish shipped all the way from Shaun Treacy's birthplace in the old country.

Treacy, big and bony and handsome as an Indian chief, treated solid day-long labor as his inheritance on earth, and brought his family of four boys and two daughters along with the same fervor. Usually friendly to a fault when he was not working, courteous as all-get-out, he was the one who invited Bracko into the barn. "Come, Jervis, and take a glorious little peek for yourself at a mighty small miracle, which may soon change of its own accord, pray the Good Lord. But while you are here, good man, best see for yourself what might damn me as a liar later on."

"What in the thundering name of heaven is that, Shaun?" Jervis said as he first looked at the colt standing in an immaculate stall of the barn. "Did you paint him yourself, man? Who has seen this sight? There'll be some strange comments coming your way, if you'll have it from me. Strange comments indeed, about some unknown but sprightly small creature from the old country itself playing games with your stock. Pity might mount itself, or stark terror that there is a new revolution here from the old land and riding on the back of a green colt. Goodness, my man, a Kelly-green colt." He swung his arms as if beseeching the very heavens above.

Treacy jumped at that. "I did nothing but bring him free of his last hold on the mare, I swear to the Almighty. In dear fact, man, it near bowled me over, for he was Kelly from the first venture into this life. Kelly green, though I think he has darkened a bit since the first day."

"How old is he now, Shaun?"

"A mere week, with strong legs and ready to run for himself, but I have kept him under covers the while, thinking he'll go brown or black before he sees the outside of the barn. A strange happening for us here, so far from the dear land of green vales and stout cliffs. My daughter Tess, dear girl born to love the animals, thinks the colt's a gift to us, to take care of, to sponsor his way in the world, whatever that may be. I swear, man, all red I could handle, or all white, or as blue as the other part of the flag, but green, Kelly-green, makes him a spectacle for most people. I fear for the young thing. If he's blest, it's one thing, but if he's pure oddity, it'll be a damned shame."

At that point, Treacy made his one and only plea to Bracko. "All I'd ask of you, Jervis, is to hold your tongue on this until we see what happens to the colt, what happens to his color. I'd not want all of Meridian City clawing around the place seeing what nature might have done to torture us or, or begorra, to please us. Nor all of the curious from here to Copa Verdi or Big Red or Clay's Pit. For that matter all of the western part of this glorious land and all the curiosity that roams as wild as the wild horses. Can I have your word on that, Jervis?" Despite all appearances and the gist of the conversation, Treacy held some consideration for the happy peddler, who had his own magic with branding irons, adding a side value of interest such as The Double-NN coming up finally as The Dublin. Treacy knew that part was devised from the onset by Bracko, part of his ingenuity. He also wondered what Bracko held in store for Cavan the Great.

"On my best honor, Shaun, on the honor of my dear departed parents. It's a mystery I am only too pleased to share with you and the family." He bowed his head in deep thinking, not sure of how to further endear himself to his usual customers along the length of his route. Or where to start. Then he said to the big Irishman, "How fares the mare, Shaun?"

Treacy shook his head, a look of bewilderment crossing his brow. "Constantly on the look for her newborn, making noise like a mother who's lost her child. I must bring them together soon, regardless of what looms ahead for us here." His clasped hands, like joined lumber peaveys, said he was in prayer for the colt.

With that encounter, they went their ways, Treacy sure he could trust Jervis Bracko not to say a word about the colt until he was as far away as he could get on his route until he started back, a six month journey. But whatever might happen, he had a witness outside the family who had seen the Kelly-green colt. He named him Cavan the Great, not Cavan the Green, but Cavan the Great. A mere half hour later, he turned loose into the back pasture the lonely mare and her sprightly colt. Treacy knew the lump in his throat was for real. The real-world beginnings for Cavan the Great had begun.

Jervis Bracko was almost two hundred miles away, about to visit the last of his customers on the long route, and his mind filled with weeks of wonder about the Kelly-green colt, Cavan. So many times, he was about to burst his gut, but business made the best decision for him. If he told his first customer coming away from The Dublin, it would spoil the rest of his trip, the whole long route out and back, and Shaun Treacy would know him for a man not true to his word, or to most of it. Plus, all the fun would fall out of his life.

And his life was full of fun, and a decent amount of hard work, just to keep things level. He had won a Springfield wagon in good condition in a bad poker game that suddenly went right for him. No idea came to mind about what to do with the wagon but, he realized, for the first time ever, he was a property owner, and he was elated. As fate happens to some people, whether they are waiting for it or not, an idea started to work in his head, and he began altering the plan of life, as he would refer to it later on.

An old handyman about town helped him to dress up the wagon and at the same time make it more useful. They put a high canvas rigging over it, provided a place for Bracko to sleep while on the road, and enough compartments and small segments to carry anything that came to mind. Hooks and nails and odd projections were added and offered many additional catch-all places to hang supplies or articles, "to temper your burdened brow, ease your troubled mind, set your best face forward for the day coming upon you, ladies." The wagon, he often said, was a rolling suitcase and he was the rolling drummer. With some insight, he became a deliverer of goods, a seller of sundries that western women would have a need for, things that would brighten their kitchens, ease their days of long labor, please their men. For the men of his route, he carried some cigars, a few choice liquors, assorted ammunition, and every now and then a small armory of side arms and rifles.

His long face-to-face with people gave him an edge in thinking and he fully realized that he needed a little more than what he carried in his wagon, an edge the good businessman needed. That, in one bright flare of light, turned out to be gossip, rumor and other like entertainment. It included white lies, bare fabrications, hyperbole to an unknown extent, and a little bit of forgery. He was an actor, elocutionist, and impersonator. And he loved it all, all part of the fun in life.

Bracko realized, as he headed into the mile-wide spread of Jocko Doherty's L-Bar-D ranch, that the stage was set for new efforts. The image of Jocko's wife Katherine swept him into the typical kitchen magic that generally came his way. The beams came on his face. The smile lighted his way in the gray morning, and Katherine Doherty, that darling lady, would be at her husband with the latest word before the day was out.

"Ah, Mrs. Doherty," Bracko siphoned from his sweet treasury, "how does the day do you? Sparkle seems the answer, the sun having risen with you no doubt, but that all should fall aside when I tell you, woman, what I have seen with my own eyes. With my own eyes, my good woman, with my own eyes. Right from the old sod and seen with my own eyes, the little people having come all this way to share with me the magic of it all. Oh, the magic of it all and all the way from the dear land itself."

As usual, Katherine Doherty melted at the sweetness of the man and the sudden realization that she would be soon possess a prize story or two from the peddler, a story of her very own.

"Oh, and a cup of tea for you, Mr. Bracko, a cup of tea and some fresh biscuits as new as the dawn and as warm." She too gleamed and beamed and immediately tasted a day's worth of talking and swapping of tales with her family and later with any neighbors that would pass by. There were some days she would beg for company, for the rattle of a wagon or the hoof beats of a horse or two. Now and then she would settle for a posse on its rounds and needing food and drink. The audience make-up made no difference.

She swung the door wide and said, "Please to come in, dear man and share your wealth with me."

And way back down the line from where his trip started, at The Dublin, Tess Treacy, as her father had bidden her, kept the mare Cavanish and her colt Cavan out at the far side of the back pasture. A small shelter had been built, water trough brought in, and a feeding bin as needed. Nobody had seen the colt but ranch hands, and all of them sworn to wait until the Kelly-green color might subside or take a turn to a normal hue.

And amid all the surprise, like a gift atop his color, the colt Cavan had the wind with him, and the longest legs and the greatest stretch of ground passing under him faster than any colt 17-year old Tess Treacy had ever seen. She loved the dear animal, right to its green coat and yellow eyes, and fed him and his dam daily with the greatest glee and happiness.

Very early in that first month, her father was moving cattle to the railhead and bent at other tasks. She first caught up to him on a quick trip home, ahead of the remuda and the trail wagon. She was pleased to see him and marveled at the energy that abounded about him.

"Pa, you will not believe how Cavan can run, so young and so fast. He'll be a champion and when he's of age I'd race him against anything born under the sun."

"Now, now, dear girl, no sense to rush at something that may never come to pass. We will keep the dear thing from general view until we know what truly has befallen him and us." But she did detect the interest and enthusiasm that was trying to find a voice, an expression.

"You do not hold to it being a miracle, Pa? Not an ounce of a miracle in it? You're from Ireland, Mother's from Ireland, Cavanish is from Ireland, and by all that's holy, Cavan is too. Straight out of Ireland. Can you not accept the fact of destiny?

"Miracles come to belief, dear Tess, to belief." His gaze found the colt at the far end of the pasture and saw that the Kelly-green had not faded, had not turned on itself. Lost for a moment in that gaze and decent reflections, he did not see but heard, from a distance, the unmistakable shout of long-time pal, Jocko Doherty. It made him smile, for Jocko Doherty was a man of both countries, the old and the new, just as he himself was… belief shrouded them, love of work and what it could produce, energy to unknown limits, and a sense of joy that life was good to him. And Jervis Bracko had accomplished a proper mission.

The hustling figure came around the corner of the ranch house. "Shaun, Shaun," came the hearty and deep voice of Jocko Doherty, "what have you done here? Where is that animal I have heard about? Do you keep him for yourself? Are you now an isolation-er in your castle, in your own private piece of royal sod? Shake him out, good man, shake him out. Show me that green Irisher." He leaned forward on his saddle, as if straining for the finish line in a race.

At the pasture fence, he came gracefully off the saddle and addressed Tess. "Dear, girl, you light up an old man's heart. Tell me quick that there is a handsome new young man in your life. You make amends for a life too old to remember." He hugged her with a grateful tenderness.

"Oh, Uncle Jocko, see what love has come in my life and she whistled with two fingers in her mouth and the colt Cavan, green as an unripe tomato, sprinted across the grass to stand at her side. Promise of strength shouted from his legs, as well as a sense of unmatched speed. And he was Tess's animal, without a doubt, as he nuzzled close to her, knew her hands on his neck.

Jocko Doherty looked with amazement on the colt shimmering in the sunlight like a piece off a flag at full mast. "Ah, Shaun, let come spring in its full glory and we will have the race of the ages, the Irisher here and my own young black beauty, Bogger, but a few months with me and of like promise. What shall we call it, Shaun, this epic match? Cavan the Great Kelly-green colt against Bogger, the black beauty from the hinterlands, descendent of the bogs of Connemara. I can see it now."

"Bye the bye, Jocko, there's but one name we can give it. One glorious name. A name for the ages. A name for all time to come so that our children will march forever to its beat, where we can ultimately rest in its good graces. We shall gather people from all over the west, the cowboys and trail hands galore, the trainmen and travelers, the adventurers and new settlers, the wild and wooly and watchful, from the Mississippi to the Rockies, from every cow town and rail head and those oddly named cities spawned by river or water head or mountain, we will pull the crowd our way and we will call the grand affair The Irish Sweepstakes. Is that not a resplendent name, old bucko? A resplendent name, The Irish Sweepstakes. Ah, begorra!"

He caught his breath and continued, his eyes afire, his cheeks as red as mountain tops at sunset. "We shall have music and flags and dancing, with a barn dance the night before and the night of the race. And great roasts all around. The best beef and steak this side of the whole long line of the Mississippi. And real potatoes in the mix of the fire, from our own seeds. Fiddlers will come from a hundred miles away, mayhap two hundred miles to play and be part of the celebration. Will that not be a fair assumption of things, my friend, a fair and grand assumption of a fair and grand time? My heart aches for the time to come."

"Ah, begorra, Shaun, you have done it well. I can feel your smooth practicality at work. You are a pride shining back on the old homesteads, and would you know it, man, not one turnip did I see on my way here. Not one turnip at all. Good lord, how do they live without turnip and the fish the curragh brought home to table? What will become of the young of them, without turnips and the good spuds and the Atlantic's largesse?"

And it was a year later, the wide spread of the great Dublin ranch ready to host an army of curious and pleasure-seeking people, much of the preliminary arrangements made and agreed upon, that Tess Treacy, in tears, burst into the kitchen. "They're gone! They're gone!"

Shaun Treacy and Jocko Doherty, at the breakfast table after a night visit by Doherty, leaped from their chairs.

"Who's gone, Tess? Who?" yelled her father.

"Cavan and Bogger. Both of them," she cried. "Gone during the night."

"How in heaven, good girl?" Doherty said, also rushing to her side.

"The barn door was open, the back door to the pasture, and the gate was down, and that's not all." The quizzical look on her face was beset with mystery, her eyes with a look of disbelief.

Shaun Treacy saw that disbelief on her face. "What else, Tess? You look all atwist, not like your good self at all. What else, girl? What else?"

Tess Treacy looked as if she was about to say something that she ought not to say, but it blurted out. "There are tracks all about, little tracks, tracks of little people, little people with little shoes. They're all around the barn and the gate and they all lead off to the pasture and to the far gate also down on the ground. I tried to trail them, but they withered away, even the tracks of Cavan and Bogger, just disappeared, as if in one stride, as if they had not been there at all."

She kept shaking her head and sobbing in the swinging change between mystery and sadness, and it was Jocko Doherty who said, "The Little People took them back. We will never see them again. Never again!"

It was the firmest statement Jocko Doherty had ever spoken. And the most believable.

Of course, Jervis Bracko ran with the tale for years on his east-west rounds. He was in hundreds and hundreds of kitchens, at the table, seated before the fireplace or the kitchen stove, on wide summer porches of an evening, talking about the Kelly-green colt and the black Bogger that were taken away by the little people. The charm spilled out of Jervis Bracko for long years and his business grew heavy and prospered and at length his children and grandchildren inherited a national merchandising chain that eventually moved on from the western territories to encompass lands on both sides of the wide Mississippi and up through the northern territories.

And Leyland Stanford, with the great horse ranch in California, sent a representative to find out the true story of the Kelly-green colt.

And so, it came down to a resolution of sorts years later, when one five-year-old great-grandson of Tess Treacy, having heard all his life the stories about the Kelly-green colt, was visiting a large fairgrounds in far Oregon. He grasped his father's hand and tried to pull him away from a hotdog vendor. "I saw my pony!" he yelled, and kept yelling it as his father was trying to complete the hotdog sale, "I saw my pony! I saw my pony!"

His father, hands full of hotdogs and change, finally said, "What pony, Cavan, what pony?" He looked apologetically at the vendor and shrugged his shoulders, and they both smiled at the boy, still caught up in exclamations.

"My green pony," he said. "My green pony that mom and grandma always told me about," and he pointed off across the fairgrounds to the merry-go-round where, in its circular and continuous path, it showed a Kelly-green horse rushing in circles and leaping high and low, and the sun shone on it like a green gem.

The Boy Who Wouldn't Eat Cheese

The boy had come out of the cave on the Island of a Thousand Rains after seven long days, his lips and cheeks drawn and pinched and his eyes yet full of darkness. Hunger sat on his face deep as a scar. Dangling from his wrists, his hands appeared thin and wiry, as if they had been unrolled from a clutch of wire, and a stumble seemed imminent and evident in his gait. Never had he remembered being so hungry, and his young body complaining all the while of aches never known before.

Now the equatorial sun burst down upon him its eternal welcome and embrace, and salt came again with its scissors of smell into his nose. Salt, proving itself once more, could cut away all things, even the unpleasant odor of his body. The cave, out of the insistent rain, had nevertheless fostered foul smells in its trade-off. But it had been warm, and dry after a fashion.

On the beach, the captain of the small ship riding out there on the quiet water, had stepped from the now-cumbersome rowboat atilt on the sand. Tall, he was, lithe in frame, with a chin a small goatee found pasture on. The eyes under the sullen and worn cap were as blue-green in their hesitancy as the sea itself, never sure which color to assume, blue for one statement, green or aqua-bent for a question, and one was forthcoming. "Are you Eduard D'Lenville? Are you the missing heir?" And then, putting his inquiry in consummate perspective, asked, "Are you the boy who will not eat cheese?"

"That's my name. That's who I am." And then, capping off his reply as if in a tiring rote, added, "That's what I do not do." Eduard D'Lenville, twelve-year old heir of a dot com fortune still rising from the garage floor of his father's former old house, lost for more than seven days on the wild Atlantic, his gait seemingly irreparable at the moment, walked toward the captain and the rowboat beached and askew on the sand. He was thinking that the man just out of the rowboat would perchance now collect a great reward. The captain was not a jaunty dresser, certainly not like his father was, now, these days, and what of such days would come back to him after all this. Clad mostly in somber gray, pants serious enough for command, a shirt with time written down into its threads, a cap the sun and wind had nearly undressed from the needle's touch, the captain delivered a serious nod to the young heir.

"You look hungry, young man, but all we have in the larder are cheese sandwiches, and wedges of cheese, between us and home port. We lost much of our supplies in the storm you also have known, and there were two other boats, those that foundered before they were righted, we had to give supplies to." He pointed back over his shoulder, to his small ship out on the sea, "And with me now are those we had to pluck from the sea and the storm that ravaged many." Over his shoulder he tossed a thumb in quick declaration.

One of the rowers, in the beached dory, waved a single hand as if to identify one soul plucked from the sea, glad to be yet of service in this world or, more to the point, merely to be in it. The waver appeared to be a bit older than the found heir, perhaps fifteen years at the most, and he waved again, a slight note of recognition in the wave, one rescued youngster saluting another rescued youngster, finding communion in sheepish grins, in the tingle of salt air.

"I am hungry. Were they all looking for me? Did my father send them?" Toward the rescued waver he looked and said, as if to each listener, but to him in particular, "I hope he did not lose any shipmates looking for me," and added a very serious nod of solicitation to his words. His eyes, so recently distant and dark when he was forlorn and bereft of hope for hours at a time, looked out on the open sea. On its flat and endless expanse, the sun was able to make solicitous angles of pleasure, the way gold or silver is fingered in the till or chest, a nickel or a dime at a time, or a dollar burst. Again, the boy thought about the reward and how this tall man, this savior clad austerely in gray and minute black, would soon have a new boat or whatever his dreams fostered up for him. Finally, as if to ward off the unnecessary dictate, implication or inference sure in any amends, to affirm his stand, he said, "But I will not eat the cheese sandwiches, or the wedges. Though I am hungry, I will not eat the cheese. It is a matter of taste with me, not honor."

The captain smiled at the boy's words as the boy walked close to him and near the boat. The boy could smell the cheese sandwiches that stood their piled decks of cards in the captain's hands, those hands openly thrust towards the boy.

Then, in bright and audible recall, the captain could clearly hear the words from the mouth of the boy's father, a likewise tall and striking man, but an alert multi-millionaire with a blue blaze in his eyes and a worry at the same time carved on his chin as though some stone mason had found it under cover, a Michelangelo at emotion.

"A handsome reward, one beyond dreams," the father had said on the porch of the great house on the promontory, his clothes now impeccably perfect, "for him who brings my son back to me, and double it if the boy eats cheese on the way home." He'd nodded then and appended a gratuitous explanation, "I handled that all wrong, giving him his leash on the meal account, bending to small dislikes, bending to whims and whimpers, the import of business too much at hand."

The captain remembered that moment, those words, as the father dropped his eyes, and his steady gaze, for making an unconscious sign as broad as a billboard. He had settled on cheese as a point of honor, though it seemed so arbitrary.

In recalling the father's words, the captain of the small boat sitting like a domino on the open sea, thought the father in error to think this boy, seven days alone on this small island, thrown from the comfort of his own small boat when mast and sail went asunder, adamant in his stance about cheese, would ever whimper. Not such a boy! Such a son I would have, thought the captain as the hungry lad fell into his arms, the whole seven days down atop him in one fell swoop. "Back to the ship to get food in his gut. Row fast, boys, the poor lad's been through the mill."

And, as luck would have it, the loose god of gods, strolling out through his universe, pointing fingers, rooting, setting storms and calms in place of choice, put about that little ship before long one more serious undertaking. The winds, more than one at a time, came out of two or three quarters; the waves rose in answer, the sea in complete abeyance cresting wildly and without rhythm, sending in motion the most irreverent energies. Calamities sailed and tossed the seas.

The little rescue ship bounced and cavorted and answered the sea's momentum and the wind's dictate. Young D'Lenville and the other young rescued boy sat side by side in the galley, crouched, dependent, anxious. That other boy's name was Andre Chabra, and both of them, teeth chattering, out of one fire and into the next one, the ship beneath them bouncing and noisy as an empty drum, held to each other for long minutes at a time. In the air a mixed stench of oil and foul food, diesel and sea fodder fighting against the clear run of salty air. Such odors are, in the gut, like a large ladle stirrer in a back-burner *olla podrida*, and both boys knew that great pot.

"I never dreamed the sea could be this mean," Andre said between drumbeats, an obvious attempt at displacement of some sort. "Is it true you have never had cheese? I love cheese. You must have tried it and *then* found out you did not like it."

The words were repetitive and forced, as if making voice for company, and almost stuck in his mouth as the ship pitched high on a crest and dipped like a roller coaster on a down grade. Pans and dishes loosely answered one another in cabinets; large pots echoed their loose habits, and grease and salt mixed in the air again and clutched anew at the innards. Andre's fine blond hair was cut in a crew fashion, his eyes gave away secrets from the back of his head, his chin never relaxing for a moment. He could have been the D'Lenville older son, so much did he look like the young heir.

"Do things happen in threes?" D'Lenville said. "Do we have a chance at another escape out of all this? Is there one more chance for each of us? The smell of cheese makes me think of old goats in a pen a long time ago, long before my father became rich. Goats are such dirty things, eating the crud of the earth. My grandmother made goats' cheese. It was horrible smelling, sticking in my head, saying foul things to me about itself, about cheese. The goat I remember most was the one with the huge udder, who dragged her teats through swill and garbage the whole day. And then my grandmother would milk her. God, it made me sick, sick as I am now, and then she'd make that awful cheese."

"Ah," Andre Chabra said, nodding an ancient's assessment, "have you not eaten the feet of pigs after their tromp in hogwash and offal and human-discarded garbage, or bacon fat, or omelet from an egg picked out of chicken shit? Meat from a scurvy lamb? Mutton sitting a week on the table in a crock, the brine heady, leading to dreams or nightmares? Had no potatoes from so close to a sump hole or cesspool or latrine the piss was barely drained away, flowed through seventeen feet of drainage it was near clean, as my grandfather used to say? They all come of the earth. They all smell of the ground that gives them life, that gives us life. Potatoes, beets, onions and scallions, yams and sweet potatoes, the rich stew of the good earth, the true yield."

About and within the ship there continued more tremendous and calamitous knocks, metal on metal, drum on drum, god on god for the comparison and the reverberations beating at their blood. The older boy collected his breath once more and continued. "You tell me you actually turn your nose up at the ground you walk on? C'mon, Eddie, get with this life, look around, not now but before or after, if we're so lucky again. Never smelled lamb kidneys cooking in oil, the spatter of butter and flour, the smell reaching down to the front hall and up to the upper apartments, like a stable was let loose, foul as hell, almost like piss call it is? Why, my Grand'Mere used to make a rouppi pie from boiled and squeezed potatoes and salt pork or chicken leftovers. You would have starved if you did not eat it. Would have starved the livelong day. My Granpere, coming down off the ladder, said it put hair on your chest and in your drawers. Aye, rouppi pie I would give up a small dream for right now; to be sitting beside her stove and gnawing away, that black chaw thick as a wad in my mouth." Odd sound effects came from his throat.

The small ship rolled again and Eduard D'Lenville, his stomach in revolt at the earthly menu of his companion, felt his guts surfacing themselves. "God, you sicken me. I feel like I will toss up what little I have in me now." He put his hand up. "Please, no more. If you want, I'll take that sandwich of cheese. I'll eat the cheese. But no more menus, please. The smell gets down inside me. It makes me worse than I am."

Andre Chabra nodded and said, "Eddie, you have no idea how much better you'll feel with something in your gut. Here," and his hand came out of his pea coat and the sandwich was there, wrapped in a scurvy-looking plastic wrapper, the yellow slice of cheese hanging from its edge like a tongue loose of its mouth. He felt the revulsion but also the threat of hunger at last come unspecified, come open armed and demand in its call.

Eduard D'Lenville, heir to a mighty fortune, chewed down the cheese sandwich, rolled with the ship as the ship rolled with the angry sea, and felt better. His older friend rolled against him in the companionship a storm brings to the sailor and shipmate. Into his gut, he had delivered the hard Earth itself, and what comes of it in the least of appointments. Taste had not delivered him, or hunger, but the cursed menu of his shipmate, the relentless dissertation on the subjective foulness of food itself, and his knowing the finicky stomach, the too-long catered-to stomach, the spoiled rotten stomach, did have a hope for generalities. The ship rolled and his gut rolled and the cheese sandwich, now in place for the very first time with him, did a slower roll and somewhat stabilized his innards. A trade-off he had made and he knew the slight benefit of it. In some neutral state he felt himself, some state of recovery.

At length, after a few hours of slap and be slapped, of gut recovery, of creaking beams and plates and bulkheads, of a loose anchor chain beating a wild rhythm and vibration that went down through the keel itself, the storm passed and the two boys at last ventured on deck. In a matter of a day and a half they were below the great promontory where the grand house of the D'Lenvilles sat like a frozen comet atop a hill. The newly rich father was elated that his son was found safe and sound, pleased that his son had at last partaken of a cheese sandwich, and cranked open his checkbook to pay off the captain.

"If you must pay him because he is the master of the boat, father, then you must pay the same to Andre Chabra here on the quarter-deck. He is the one who got me to send over my folly, who got me to eat the first cheese sandwich, to remember grandmother's goat and not get sick again. Andre cured me. Andre deserves a great reward too, and he will buy a new boat and he and I will sail it when we are ready, for we have been to the sea and the sea has found us favorable. She has taken us and given us back, cheese be damned, the old goat be damned.

And the newly rich father poured out from his rich coffers a double reward and knew that his son was a survivor, that the sea had another conscription to its credit. And Eduard D'Lenville and Andre Chabra sailed for years on their own boat, and were sailing long after the dotcom fortune of the senior D'Lenville had disappeared in the dust and the goats were left well behind the last landfall of each voyage.

The sea, like secrets, is deeper than we know.

Ankton the Glass Man and the Boy Who Threw Stones at Trees

Out past everything, where endings and beginnings get mixed up, Ankton the Glass Man lived. He liked his place because he did not have to share the little he had with people because there was little he had to give. His house was a very minor house of one room that had bed and stove at opposite sides and not much in between. But Ankton was a happy man who could make the fire sing and glass take turns on itself.

In the town a way from him, The Town Whose Streets Had No Names, lived a sad boy. He was sad because he had no hobbies or no activities that he was good at. He lived in an apartment above the sweet shop, on The Street Where the Sweet Shop Is. Many times, Ankton would look up and see the boy coming down the road to visit his shop. Ankton could tell it was The Boy Who Lived Above the Sweet Shop because he was always kicking things in the road or throwing stones. Most often the boy, in a very special way, would pick up a stone and pick out a target and toss the stone at the target. Mostly it was trees he threw at.

The Boy Who Lived Above the Sweet Shop liked to watch Ankton the Glass Man work. And he came to visit very often, but often brought his sadness with him. "Why does the glass curl like that?" he'd say when Ankton was curving the neck of a glass bird for The Woman Who Lived Beside the Church on The Street Where the Church Is. The boy's face was full of wonder as well as sadness.

"Why are you so sad, my young friend?" Ankton said one day.

"Because I cannot sing like some of my friends or play a horn or the piano like some of my friends. One friend knows how to whittle already. His grandfather taught him and now his grandfather has died.

My other friend who lives on The Road Where the Pond Is can whistle a hundred songs and I can't even carry a tune. I don't know what the mystery of music is. It does not fill my head like it must fill his head."

"What is your name?" Ankton said one day when the boy was tossing stones across the road at a tree. The sound kept coming back from across the road when each stone hit the tree.

"My name is Arvell. I am named after my grandfather who could not do anything either. He just cut wood in the forest. Anybody can cut wood in the forest. The man who lives on the Street Where the Bakery Is cuts wood and everybody knows that's all he can do. It's so easy. Just like the men who haul the wood into town to the mill. They are just like donkeys or mules."

"What does your father do?" Ankton said one day as he spread the beautiful wings of a blue bird. Heat rose from the wings as if from the heart of the fire. The boy Arvell sighed when he saw the span of the wings and the light of the sun passing like magic through the wings. And his breath caught in his throat as Ankton folded the wings back in another push at flight for the blue bird. Arvell said to himself that he saw feathers. He was certain of it. It made him happy, but it made him sad too. He fired six stones at the tree across the Road Where the Glass Man Lives.

"My father went away to be a soldier and never came back," Arvell said. "He was probably not a very good soldier." There were no tears in his eyes.

"When he was here, he could only dig in the ground. He dug holes for people who wanted to build houses. All he could do was shovel dirt. It does not take much to dig dirt. It's not like practicing to be good or taking lessons from a master. It's not like playing a piano or even a harmonica. Oh," he added, firing more stones at the tree, "if only I could play the harmonica. Everybody would know me. I would play it on Saturdays in my back yard or sitting on the steps. I would play it going to school. People would say *There Goes the Boy Who Plays the Harmonica.* I would be happy then."

Arvell the sad boy fired six more stones across the Road Where the Glass Man Lives. Ankton heard the sounds of the stones hitting the tree. It sounded like "Thrack!" Six times he counted "Thrack!" and smiled to himself. It was as if he were hearing music.

For he too, like Arvell, could not carry a tune in his head, so he made music out of all the "Thracks!" he ever heard. And the trains that said "Thrump" in the far night or "Clack-thrip, clack-thrip," all the time they circled The Town Whose Streets Have No Names. The music he knew hummed around him all the time, just waiting to be caught.

One day the wings of another glass bird soared above Ankton's head where he held it frozen in flight. Sunlight danced through the veins in the bird's wings. He heard "Clack-thrip, Clack-thrip," from a new train, and more "Thracks!" from Arvell's sure aim.

And finally, one day, the boy tossing the stones stood at length in the back of Ankton's mind. The boy was frozen there in his mind, frozen in place so that nothing in the whole world could disturb it. He could measure the boy's arm and see how his head set itself as he took aim at a tree. The position of his feet as the boy threw the stones was always the same, was always like hitting the same note on the piano. Every single time it was perfectly in the same position. All the way out from town he could see the boy in his mind, how his arm would fling out stones in perfect flight, how the stones flew like his own birds, in a flight that is best at imagining. The blue bird and a red bird and a great eagle and a great wingspread hawk with open fingertips of feathers leaped from an invisible thermal into his mind.

All these things were locked in Ankton's head. And came the day when Arvell, The Boy Who Threw Stones at Trees, who came from The Town Whose Streets Have No Names, came out of the fire, leaped as if he had wings of the blue bird or the great hawk, came out of a mass of glass as pure as any idea could be. One would swear the boy's arm was about to hurl a stone with unerring accuracy at a twig of a slight tree that sat all the way across the road.

The sad boy Arvell came and saw the sunlight passing with dazzle through The Boy Who Threw Stones at Trees. He counted the ways the light bounced through the glass with a great sense of energy. He saw how dazzle and gleam and motion could all be caught up at one time. His breath was taken away, for he saw what he was, he saw how this master glass man looked at him and made an image that was frozen forever in time.

And he finally realized his father was a hero, that woodcutters and earth diggers are as necessary as doctors or piano players, that the glass man was the smartest man who ever lived, the glass man who knew The Boy Who Threw Stones at Trees would become the Greatest Pitcher Baseball Has Ever Known.

We all know it wasn't Babe Ruth.

The Man Who Hid Music

One day at the little house where the dowser used to live, a kind-looking man with a beard came carrying all he owned on an A-frame on his back. He set the A-frame on the ground and looked at the small house needing much work. Muscles moved under his shirt." Whose house is this?" he said to some children playing at an edge of a field. This was the place where the mountain came to a rest, but the river had not been found as yet.

One of the boys said, "It used to belong to the dowser, but he went away." The boy used a stick to walk with as one leg was slightly crooked and made him lean.

"Why did he go away?" the man said, looking closely at the stick the boy had to use.

"People laughed at him," answered the boy. When he looked at his friends some of them began to chuckle and grin. "Don't," the boy said. His sandy hair caught the wind; his eyes were hazel and steady.

"If I want to fix this house up and live here, tell me who I have to see." The children could see some of the tools hanging on the man's A-frame. On edges where the sun touched them, the tools shone brightly as if they had been polished with gems.

"See Macklow the mayor. He lives down there where those walls meet." The boy pointed across the wide fields. "He'll be on his porch listening to the birds of the fields. My name is Max. What is your name?"

The man of the tools smiled at Max's description of the mayor. "My name does not count, only what I do," he said. He walked across the fields and soon had the house to work on. At first it was just the children who watched him fix doors and steps and windows, but soon other people, including Macklow, came to watch. All the time he used tools the man whistled different tunes. At his work, he was a happy man.

The house was soon a sparkling and cozy place with no lopsided boards and no broken steps and no windows free to the air. When the man needed wood, he put the empty A-frame across his shoulders and walked off toward the mountain and the forests. In the evening, he returned with a pile of wood of all lengths sitting across the back of his shoulders.

"Someday, perhaps soon," he said one day to the children watching him, and a few of the older people, "I will have a surprise for you." As usual, just at dusk, the man took some of his wood he had been working with and brought it inside the little house. The light went on inside so they knew he was still working.

Nobody knew what he was working on. But the light burned long into many nights.

And soon, to everyone's surprise, a garden was also blooming behind the house. Macklow was really surprised because his own fields were slow. Nobody had seen the kindly man walk out of his little house at night, time after time, and put buckets of water on his little garden. The dowser's well was right inside the little house and those who had laughed at the dowser never knew about the well and the sweet water it gave up.

One morning the man came out of his house and gave a new stick to Max. It was much better that Max's old stick, and was smooth and polished and very strong. Max was proud of his new stick and could walk faster with it. Over his head he waved it and showed it off to his friends.

On each morning from then on, the man began to build a fence around the house and the garden. At first, he put up strong posts, then mounted stringers between the posts.

When all the posts and stringers were mounted and connected, he began to place upright pickets on the stringers.

Now and then one of the pickets would cause someone to laugh and titter about its strange shape. Some of the pickets were not as pretty and straight as others. Some indeed looked odd and out of place. But the man kept adding both straight and odd-looking pickets to the fence.

"See," Macklow said one day when village people were talking about the fence, "he brings out what he brought into the house the night before. What he does to it is a mystery, but let us not laugh at him. We laughed at the dowser and he went away in the night. This man is a kind man and has promised us a surprise. Do not laugh at him, no matter what his fence looks like."

When he looked at little Max with the new stick, Max and Macklow swapped nods, as if they shared a secret.

But laughter, though, did come each day, at the way the fence looked, at crooked or bent pickets, at the weird shapes of some of them.

Then the day came when all the vegetables in the garden were ripe and the bizarre fence circled the house. The man seemed pleased and put his tools down except for one knife and walked off toward the forest. He came back with one small piece of wood. From that piece of wood, he whittled a small whistle. When he blew into the whistle, he found only one note, a pure note, but only one note.

There was more small laughter and chuckling, but Macklow, remembering the dowser, thinking about the new ripe garden and his own slow crops, would not laugh. Nor would Max with his new walking stick. One morning the man spoke to some people looking at his crop and studying what he had done to fix the house and the fence he had placed all around it. "I have hidden the music here. Music is a part of the soul. Music is part of the water too. And water is part of the soul.

Whoever finds the music I have hidden can have this house, for Macklow says it is mine to give."

Macklow nodded his head.

In the morning the man was gone. The tools were gone. The A-frame was gone.

People pored over the house trying to find the music. They did not know what they were looking for. But they found the dowser's well at the back end of the house and wondered at that. Macklow marveled at the well. However, he made sure none of them disturbed the things the man had done to fix the house.

It was curious. Nobody could find the music. None of them knew what they were looking for. But Max kept playing the whistle and kept hearing the note. He would sit on the porch and blow the whistle until people began to be bothered by it and asked him to stop.

But Max also knew that note deep inside his head.

For weeks people looked for the music. But they did not know what they were looking for.

And then, one morning as he walked past the house, Max hit one of the pickets with his stick.

Oh, how his heart pounded in his chest. How it grew it seemed that it might explode.

It was the same note from the whistle. The exact same, beautiful note.

Back to the gate he went, at the same note-sounding picket and began to walk around the house, his stick slapping against each picket in turn, the way boys have done ever since going by church and school yard fences.

And Macklow looked and the people looked and they all heard the music coming from the fence pickets as Max, walking without his stick support for the first time in his life, played elegant music on the ugly looking pickets with the stick the man had carved. The circled fence played out a whole lovely tune.

And Macklow saw to it that Max and his mother had themselves a new house to live in, at the place where the mountain comes to rest and the river is not yet found.

Pianos and viola strings now and then have odd company at the platform.

The Man with the Broken Crutch

It was where the Dark Forest runs out of breath and the river, pretending to be thief, steals much of daylight's silver. It was here one morning, the man with a broken crutch came out of the forest and came along the river gathering its coin. He wore a cap for the weather and a jacket time had touched roughly. And he limped.

The limp was a serious limp, almost twisting the man's frame. The object foot had a dragging stutter to it and the boot was greatly worn. The man promised to topple easily. And need or want moved in the air about him.

The single crutch at his left side was a crude apparatus, bound in places where it had been broken with wire tightly coiled. Avershaw the blacksmith, from his porch, saw him first, noticed how he leaned to one side. "Melba," he called, and his wife came onto the porch. "We will have another for breakfast I am sure." Her apron was gathered in her hands and she looked at the stranger and said, "I am sure we will."

Avershaw, a big man with red suspenders and heavy pants, stood and hailed the other man. "Would you stand for coffee and a biscuit, sir? We do not have abundance, but we have sufficient. Eggs would be another matter." Again, Avershaw noted how the man leaned almost to the point of falling. Then he noted the kindly face, the clear blue eyes, the way the man held his chin. And his hands! His hands were delicate and smooth and did not look as if they belonged with the crutch or had much employed the crutch.

"You are too kind, sir," the man with the crutch said. A slight smile wore on his face. "We are in luck, for I have two eggs here I found last evening in the forest, and no place to cook them." From a pocket of the worn jacket he brought out two brown eggs that could be yet idling in a nest. "If the lady of the house would oblige, she may do as she wishes with them." His hand held out the two brown eggs and Avershaw called his wife. "Melba, we'll have biscuits dipped in eggs today, just the way you like them."

Then Avershaw pointed to a chair and said, "Rest easy while the biscuits get dipped and fried. We'll have our coffee here where the sun comes first. If I were a wood smith, I would fix that crutch for you, but my iron would be too heavy for you." Then Avershaw said, "By what name are you called, sir?"

They call me Stick. They have called me Stick for a long time, for so long I know no other name. So, Stick I will be. It is not uncomfortable."

They had their biscuits with a small mound of butter and sweet syrup. And a second cup of coffee.

"Do you have far to go?" Avershaw said, as he finished his coffee. "We could put some lunch in a kit for you."

"Not far," Stick said, "not far at all."

When the coffee was gone Stick said thank you and went on his way.

Just before noon, still where the forest runs out of breath and the river steals daylight, Stick was hailed by another man in his front yard. The man had seen that serious limp in the heat of the sun. "Stranger, would a bit of shade and a small bite of food aid you on your journey? We do not have much but we will share. I am with my two daughters. Today is a day without meat for us. We have but few pennies left from what bread we could buy."

"Such a lucky day it is," Stick said. "Last night in the forest I came upon a deer who had shortly impaled himself. I came away with some venison." From deep in his jacket pocket, he drew out a small parcel wrapped in paper. "However your daughters choose to cook it, be it done." The daughters danced away with the venison. Soon the aroma climbed on the air in the middle of the day. There was a sauce to go with the bread and the four of them dipped their bread and ate the venison.

"My name is Rastoff and I teach music," Rastoff said, his big teeth showing as he talked. "If I could work with wood, I would make you a new crutch to aid in your journey. But I have no knowledge of wood. Nor what its grain is or where its strength lies, except here." And with that he drew a violin up from below the table and played songs for Stick and his daughters. After a while, Stick said, "I must be going. But I do not have far to travel." He left with his *thank you* as soft as music on the air.

Stick was not far away by the close of evening. A boy came up to him and said, "My mother saw you coming for a long time from her window. We do not have much but you are welcome to be at our table. We have soup. It is thin, but it will be warm."

"Young man," Stick said, "tell your mother we are in luck. Just last evening, in the middle of the Dark Forest, where there was a small patch of late sunlight, I found two potatoes, two beets and two carrots." He dug deep into his jacket pocket and brought out the vegetables. "Tell your mother to thicken the soup with these."

The boy nodded with delight and ran off to give the vegetables to his mother. He soon came back and said, "She thanks you a great deal. If my father were here, he could fix your crutch for you, but he is away in the Great War that moves around the world. We hope he comes back soon. He is a carpenter and could fix your crutch easily."

At dusk they ate the newly thickened soup with the potatoes and the beets and the carrots cut up in it. The soup was delicious soup and the boy soon fell asleep on the porch of his house while the mother cleaned the dishes. Stick said goodbye. "I have to keep moving. You have a fine boy. I hope your husband gets back soon. War is a great separator but often not the final one."

His way took him along a stone wall for a few miles.

The river had nearly given up all of its daylight, when Stick was walking past an old farmhouse sitting like a deep shadow. Not one window had a light in it, nor was there any smoke coming from the chimney. A voice hailed him from the darkness in front of the house. "If you have no place to sleep, sir, we could put you up, but you must be able to do with the darkness and the cold. We do not have any light or any kindling to start a fire or any matches for the matter. I am afraid that my children will not be able to do their reading this night and they might also catch cold. The edge of the moon says it is going to be cold."

"You are most kind, sir," Stick said, "but fear not. Last evening in the forest I found some flint and stone in an old pouch on a tree stump. We can start a fire with them."

"All well and good," the man in the darkness said, "but we still have no kindling to get the big logs burning."

"Ah, but we do, "Stick said, as he slammed his broken crutch over a large stone in the wall and splintered it for kindling. The sound crackled so harshly in the night it frightened the man.

"But how will you walk on the morrow?" the man said.

Stick had no hesitation. "You will make me a crutch tonight," he replied.

"I have been unable to work for a long time," the man said. But all night he worked hard on some pieces of wood he found, knowing that before this stranger came, he would not have even looked for such wood. Light came from a good fire and warmth filled the house and the children were asleep after reading their lessons. In the morning, the man handed Stick a shiny new crutch that caught the early morning sun all along the shaft. The crutch was smooth and had a lacquer finish on it and a pad on the top where it fit under Stick's arm.

That sun was barely up over the horizon when Stick walked away in the early slant of the sunlight, down past the fields he went, past the stone walls, to where the river again was catching up all the daylight it could grasp. Once, he waved back at the man with his new crutch.

That evening all the people had gathered in town and were talking about the man with the broken crutch.

"I am glad that we were able to feed him," Avershaw said, his thumbs hooked on his red suspenders. "We gave him breakfast, a royal breakfast, a meal to begin the day with." He paused, hooking his suspenders a little higher. "As my mother used to say,

'A meal to touch the backbone.'"

"And we gave the poor man his lunch," Rastoff said, "with venison and thick gravy. A meal also fit for a king." He smiled proudly, his large teeth showing. "We even played music for him to soothe his vagrant soul. If there were a place for that poor man to live, this would be it. We all did so much for him. All taking our turn with a stranger." Those around him nodded in agreement.

The boy's mother, not to be outdone, not wanting to be left out of a share of goodness, took her turn. "A most splendid and thick soup we gave the man. Thick as can be, with potatoes and beets and new carrots. A treat for any beggar on his rounds. The kind that sticks to one's ribs." It was a kind of punctuation when she added, "And he ate a goodly share of it."

The others nodded in agreement again, seemingly all of one mind.

They were satisfied with themselves, but a voice from the edge of light, the man from the darkness, said, "Do any of you know what he gave to us? Why do we continually wrap ourselves up in our own gifts? Why do we tie up our own ribbons in such a manner?"

"Well," the boy's mother said, "what did you do for him? It was near dark when he left my house."

"What fools we are," the man answered. "It's not what we did for him. It's what he did for us. He took care of us. Me, a useless man for years, I made a crutch for him. I haven't worked like that in a long time and I guess we all know that." For a moment he hung his head. "That's one of the reasons he came here. The man needed a crutch to get on with. And he saw to it that I made it for him. We did not really do for him. He did for us, but we are afraid to say it."

The next morning, on the other side of the river, where the mountain comes to stand up and the field stops breathing, a man with a broken crutch came limping out of the forest ready to lean on some more people.

A man hailed him from his porch.

The Old Man Who Whittled Whistles

In a country that had no name because it had no borders lived an old man who lived in a small cabin at the side of the road and spent all his days whittling whistles, his knife a magic implement in aged hands. For starters, all he ever wanted to do, from the day he was gifted a special knife, was to carve or whittle whistles that would possess and emit on demand special notes, special songs. Each time he made a whistle and tested it, he would make a present of it for a boy or girl who passed his small house. Hundreds of youngsters of all ages arrived at his doorstep over the years and often walked away with a whistle when one was ready for whistling.

The story of the whistle man became legend, and people in all directions knew about him.

Lucky youngsters, at such moments, danced away with glee and the echoes of their newly-carved whistles would come back from some distance to please the old man, a music floating in the air, touching his spirit, often, with surprise, reaching back into long memories he had not opened in moons upon moons. Such small pleasures, often faint but real, were true delicacies for him, images galore, tunes resplendent.

This long-range touching was important to him, as he was partially crippled in his legs that stuck like tree limbs on an odd growth tree, though he never once, in all the times he has been busy at whittling, ever cried about his personal circumstances, or what brought him to such a condition. His name, which he never treated with any importance, was Evan Thurble, and he presented a strangely but comfortable appearance in knickers pants, bearing a herring-bone pattern in a pale green color, a tunic with short sleeves that ended at his elbows as though they had been chopped off in a rough manner, for they were ragged at the edges, though evinced no great discomfort, and a small, barely visible insignia of an unknown origin.

The old man entertained no big dreams and harbored no thoughts of grandeur. His house, to situate this tale, was a small house and once the forest behind his house had been thick and heavy with trees. Now, after these busy days, the long years at his sole occupation, it was sparser because of all the whistles he had whittled out of its trees; often one limb of a giant tree disappearing in a single season.

It was well known that boys and girls everywhere played his whistles. But the thinning forest continued to have nice shade and was a fine place to walk, and bright spring brought new growth, new promise and, of course, new whistles.

Joy, it seemed, was everywhere about him for he knew spring was a celebration of the grandest order; new buds, new blossoms, new green grass that could run for miles

Each mornin, the man would sit on his rocker on the porch and listen to the birds, small flocks of them, and then wing-spread hundreds of them, generally at high chorus. When the light of day came upon them, they began to whistle and send out signals to their brethren and friends. Very closely he would listen, picking up every sound that limped or leaped came out of the forest. He heard every peep and every chirp and there never was a bird's song that he did not hear from one magnificent note to the next and on to the last note of the delivery. After long moments of listening he would settle on a sound or a song that best suited him for the day. He would set off for the forest to find a piece of wood to whittle to capture those sounds forever.

In the forest came a kind of magic with the old man's search for the right piece of wood. It was without fail that he'd find the right piece. It could be sitting in its place as a nice branch on a maple tree or it could be a strip of oak that lightning had driven away from its home at the top of a tree. Now and then, it would be the shape of a piece of wood that caught his eye instead of his ear. But it was always the right piece. It was as though all things performed in collaboration to secure his search for a most promising piece of wood, for the nonce idle in its existence, though new promise was extant in the forest.

And he always gave away the whistles he made to children.

Oh, how he loved new songs the birds whistled, and he could tell practically which day of the year it was, the day of the season, because of the birds that stayed or the ones that already had journeyed far away. Some of the birds would end up way down in the other end of the world and would be gone for months. Some little red birds stayed all year long, singing songs for the old man. He loved the ones who stayed and the ones who traveled, loved none more than the other.

One day, spring warm as a reflection, when he was sleeping deeply in his late afternoon nap, a bad man rose surreptitiously from late day's gray shadows and stole the old man's knife as it lay exposed on his small work bench. The thief slipped away on soft shoes and with every caution imaginable. How sad the old man became. How sad the children were when no whistles were being made. Someone in town said the birds, in their own support, had stopped singing, proving the forest sometimes could be a dark, dismal and too quiet a place able to frighten even a robust soul.

The leaves, likely overnight, began to fall in the forest. Cool and then cooler winds twisted out of the north and the northeast in shrieks and turns in their own alarm-clock fashion, The pleasant temperatures of firm bodies and structures began to decline as full shadows took over this end of the Earth.

And then, the snow began to fall on a calamitous day before November was even a week old, which set old men on corners into rumbling and grumbling conversations. "You ever feel the likes of this at this time of year, Palmer? In 80 and odd, I never did, and old Patterson at the railroad station, got me by a month, argues that way too. Says he's about to pull his wooler out of the closet. 'Magine that."

And old man Thurble was sadder each day he could not whittle. Even faint smiles would not light his face, and his cheeks and his belly began to puff with unneeded weight from his lack of exercise and his own regular trips into the heart of the forest, even on the hottest days of the year.

Then, one bright morning, the son making a climatic entry on its own, a new knife was placed by an unknown hand on the whittler's porch. The old man did not know who left it there. But he suddenly heard, full of life and newness, overhead, abounding and loose and free as ever, a singular and effervescent bird call from the forest. Out he went and found a piece of wood exactly as he thought it should be. The whistle came to its bounden life in Thurble's hands with the new knife and caught the new birdcall perfectly, whereupon he hung the whistle on his fence.

All the long day, with a sense of anxiety, and locked in a quandary, he saw the new whistle untouched by one child; it hung as if imprisoned out in the open.

But all the boys and girls in all directions knew in quick order what had happened because of the new knife in the hands of the old man and none of them took the newest whistle away from the fence. That made the old timers talk, too. "They ain't scared a bit, Palmer, but they's a story cotton on to it, mark my words."

Next day the old man heard another bird and made another whistle and hung that one on his fence. But no one took it. He was sad, but making whistles was what he always wanted to do, so he kept at it.

The birds, the autumn birds and the winter birds still hanging about, kept calling and he kept making whistles and he kept hanging them on his fence. And still, nobody came to take the whistles. The fence grew greatly, one whistle after another going into place, the snow coming, the snow going, spring in its new leap.

Day after day, for the longest time, amidst seasonal hardships, he heard the birds and made his whistles and hung them for the boys and girls. Each night he was sad when he saw them all remaining in place. But he knew he would never stop making whistles. Birds were beautiful when they sang and his whistles were beautiful when they were played and somehow someday someone would come along to play lovely tunes on the small shafts of wood.

Soon there were hundreds of whistles hanging on his fence and not a single one had been taken. No boy or girl ever tried to play one or blow air into the mouthpiece or even tried to finger the little air holes. Not a single boy or girl tried one out. It was if they all were cautioned by the theft of his first knife. And not one whistle disappeared in the middle of the night or found an ornery hand.

Not a single one.

And it was late that winter the old man became sick and lay in his bed and the mayor and some other people came from the town when they heard about his trouble. And the old man told them his life had been a good life and he had no regrets except that he wished the boys and girls would come to take his whistles off the fence. But even if they don't, he had said, he had been happy making his whistles.

And then, late in the afternoon, the wind began to blow from the edge of the forest. It blew quickly and steadily down the length of the old man's fence. The old man and the mayor and many other people suddenly heard the most marvelous sounds they had ever heard, the most magical notes of every range imaginable, as if from a heavenly source to be remembered forever, and not by chance the music from the soul of one old man who had found the secret of songs.

And before that windy selection was over, before the last soft note was sent on its way, the old man who made whistles all his life finally and happily closed his eyes as he heard music coming from the very first fence organ ever played.

Notes are often passed in secret between the players.

The Star Blitz

Treasure there was someplace in life, at your feet if you stopped to breathe, around the corner if you turned it the right way at the right moment, at the end of a quiet lane you might find yourself in by accident. Of this Tony Falcone was sure. Absolutely sure! Two things rang true about Tony Falcone from the very first word said of him, he drank inordinately, excessively, purportedly without care, and he dreamed the same way, full-blown, full-scale dreams, wide, ambitious, Mississippian, artistic no less, and with an inveterate regality.

His father had said to him one day when Tony was just a boy with a very minor attention span, advice which he remembered just about every day of his life (at least sober, and part way to that other place he inhabited so often), "Dream all you want, son, dream like you might be king, which you won't be, but they can't take it away from you; just don't do it crossing the street or walking down the railroad tracks. Pay all your dues as they come up, crow a little bit when in luck, shut up when you lose, but dream all you want. It might just become the biggest pleasure of your life. There are worse things to hold onto."

His father was only half right in his advice. There were the dreams, the endless and rich flow of them; and there was the mesmerizing bottle, the endless temptation somehow just a little too much each time for him. That, too, was dream-stuff of another order, a whole magical elixir which, inexplicably, came to be in itself both cause and effect, end of a means and means to an end, a thing by and for itself. What else it gnawed at, licked its chops over, was all of time.

He had come, thus, into his thirty-seventh year, a bachelor cut right out of the drinker's mold, a bit shaggy most of the time, starting to thin in his hair, eyes clear only slightly more than half the day, as a town laborer his hands callused by pick and shovel, his back still showing ridges of muscle not yet worn down in their due, but, above all of this, indisputably, he was an Earthmover of the first measure. Tony Falcone did not call himself a laborer or a shoveler, not a handyman hidden under another title, but Earthmover. Not two words, but one word, rolled up into its cosmic greatness, its spatial and glorious reach. He had dreamed it into existence, into place. No foreman or job super, and no peer could take it away from him. Earthmover he was and Earthmover he would remain.

Eddie Wiggins, tea tippler extraordinaire, brass rail bucko of the first order, current co-owner of the trench they were at the moment excavating under the hot August sun, flung a shovelful of gravel high, wide and handsomely to the other side of the pile and said, to Tony and the massive sense of oppression hanging like hate in the air, ""I'd give my best arm for a cold one right now, Tony. A frosted glass, a bottle with ice still clinging to it, sliding slowly down the side of the glass, slippery, oozing, cold as the fires of hell when they are long out. What the hell time is it?"

His dry tongue rode around the orbit of his dry lips, raspy, abrasive, catching on high dry spots. His beard was a day and a half old. Sandy hair he had, full of moisture the sunlight kept catching hold of. The large and awesomely veined hands spread about the shovel handle seemed sculpted out of a blue-red granite, the veins as vivid as tattoos. Thickly square on the ends, his fingernails looked as if they had been abraded by a rugged rasp. One might have called him handsome, but no one, after a second look, would have called him out of place in the trench.

In his best friend's face, Tony could see a bit of the hangdog holding forth. Did his own eyes have that same look in them, the last mile look, an also-ran look, their assurance and the day itself practically shot to hell already, and it not yet three p.m.? He decided very quickly that they did. If he had looked sharper, he knew he would have seen it a lot earlier. Hell! He would have seen a lot of things a lot earlier, but what the hell makes time so special now, now when all the dyes are cast.

He'd kept saying that to himself for so long it seemed that it must have preceded anything being wrong in his life in the first place. Effect coming ahead of the cause. He tried to think that over and decided to take a huge shovelful on his next scoop, it was easier that way; the body allowed so much relief of itself, for itself, and that included the mind. Such an out! Giddiness, a surge of joy he knew was temporary at its absolute best, flowed through him. The bright, flashing tip of the shovel slammed into the earth, cocked itself almost at once under a measure of hardpan and gravel he thought no man could possibly dredge up, and then the body pitch and sense of timing came geared together smoother than the best wine could ever be, or ever do. A definite knack was required of all this, that was for damn sure.

For the briefest moment, he was partly relocated down the street, on a high limb of a tree looking back at himself in the trench, seeing himself for what he was and where he was and what he was doing. The shovel, came his immediate response, was no different than a scalpel. Surgeons, too, did their digging, didn't they? Down through the matter of the body and the brain, clawing and pawing and ultimately finessing their way through to some resolution, some appointment in the narrowness of spaces, just as he was here in earth's open aorta, this passage across the face of the earth, this single line of a massive network that would never be fully measured. Struggling in his mind was the idea of eternity and the plane he was currently on extending itself out into space and into limitless time. Being a part of that plane was important; on a pedestal or in a ditch, makes no difference, you can extend yourself only so far out on that limitlessness.

All of it hit him, as it often did, but there was no getting away from it; here in this life, locked to this place, he drank, he dreamed, he knew it, and nothing was going to change it. That was one sure thing in life, and having anything that was a certainty was often a joy to hold to one's self. One could grab onto a certainty. Could almost wear it. Toga. Mantle. Robe. A cover against most anything. Better than a body bag, for sure, or a poncho looped about you in war's action, in the rain, in a far land.

Again, looking at his companion in the trench, fellow Earthmover on the face of the earth, color and complexion added to that assessment as he noted the redness pervading his friend's face. Eddie's, as usual here in the late noon of the day, was brick red, partly due to sunlight and partly due to whatever it was they had managed to knock off the night before. There had been bottles and glasses and kegs and cans and liquid movement for much of the night, and he couldn't remember past one certain point; when they had the argument about hidden treasure on Vinegar Hill.

He had yelled at Eddie. "Damn fool drunk! What do you think old man Haskell and his kid have been digging up there for these thirty-five years? Not for their health, I tell you. They know something, trying to keep it from us. I keep seeing a box at the end of my shovel, a metal box, the pot at the end of the rainbow, and I know it's full of gold and jewels and enough other crap to knock our eyes out. Every day of my life I've dreamed of it, even before I knew they were digging up there. I hear the sounds that come with it, the sound my shovel makes at contact, the squeak of old hinges trying their wings once again, the spill of such shining you couldn't imagine in a hundred years. We could lie on the beach until our last drink had its way with us. I tell you, Eddie, there's something up there, and they know it, and we know it. The stupidest thing we could do is to just plain forget about it. That'd really scratch a lifetime."

"You dream too much, Tony, my friend." His voice was thick and tortured in a sense, as if words were being squeezed out of him. Resting one foot on the heel of the blade, he leaned on his shovel. His chin sat on the tip of the shovel handle, posing him part Atlas. Tony knew he'd remember his friend that way forever, whenever that came, as Eddie continued: "You stare out at space all day like you expect to see a star. You're never going to see a single one in the daytime, so why look?

101

Then, the way you always do, getting loose or getting tight, I don't know which it is, you turn around and stare at the ground under your damn feet like you're in some holy place, or like something's going to pop up in your face you've been waiting for. It's just not going to happen like that, Tony. Things don't go that way for us. All that stuff is way, way beyond us. We're in our place, come hell or high water. We dug our way in. There's no way out for us."

There was a basic finality to his words, one without question, as if all had been drafted and done long before them, cut, shucked and dried. He added a closer he thought would be a telling one, "And, besides, you think too damn much! All the time thinking!"

Nothing new in those words; he'd said them before and most likely would say them again. A smile was offered with that pronouncement, a half smile of instant neutrality, of taking back a piece of what had been said.

Tony smiled too, realizing he had just gone through the old argument. It must be a sign of our desperate straits, he thought, or our universal acceptance of being where we are and what we are.

"But I'd still rather have a drink, too!" There was, appreciatively, nearly a kind of music and rhythm to his voice as the phrase sounded slowly in his ear, at the back of his head, at some hollow place he had no control over, indeed where much odd conversation took place in the accompaniment of spirits. Almost a song, he said under his breath. A thousand times he had uttered that phrase, and knew it was a part of him. Against the current obstacles he managed to wet his tongue, remembering, tasting.

Everything didn't have to be so cut and dried, did it? A laugh began in his throat, as he found appreciation for his own humor.

"I'm going up there after work tonight, Eddie, and if you don't want to come with me, that's okay. But I'm going. Soon's they're are out of there, I'm up there." He let it sink right in with his friend, who, he knew, could never take the chance that he might come up with something, something big.

The bottles purchased had been dirt cheap, a Muscatel they sort of withdrew to when finances demanded. Before evening they were well into the storied steps of the bottles, Tony's tales at last charming and mesmerizing Eddie so that he agreed to make the climb up Vinegar Hill, "Come hell or high water". They would have celebrated, but they were already primed at partying.

The climb up Vinegar Hill was not without incident; Eddie falling a number of times, yelling out in the poor light that he might be damned to death for what he was trying, trespassing on somebody else's private dreamland. Tasting dirt was not his favorite outing at any time, and here he was, out of the trench he had spent his day in, and still locked into the taste of old earth, all of loam and gravel and hardpan; Tony, finding it clumsy to tote the extra fuel for lamps he had determined they would need, because the Haskells never worked late hours.

Once, in his protracted agony, he fell face down in the path, cursing at first the whole mountainside, finally managing a laugh only Eddie could understand and decipher, and he'd bet on that, he'd bet the farm on that, whatever damn farm that would be in all of creation. A drunk's laugh only another drunk would understand, all the stress sound and punctuation in place. Believing for the moment that he was only slightly dizzy, he suddenly felt the affinity that brothers have, sharers, fellow sufferers; it cut right into him, a full presence, a knowledge once put aside would not be brought back to light, but if accepted, came down on a man hard as an avalanche. Life came down with it, heavy as rocks, the tumble of agony and truth, the big bang of reality trying to get its way into the slightest crevice of his mind. He felt the penetration of, at once, despair and truth, fact and fiction, loss the likes of which he had never known. The gold nuggets, the storied and dreamed nuggets, like the hard yellow of lifesavers, came once again to fill his mind, the gold nuggets and bright silver by the bucket, and stones so precious in life they had entities of their own, and coin so varied in size and so crude in inscription he never would know its meaning.

He saw the words tumble from the corner of his eyes, the flash across the coming coins, the words even before they were in his eyes—their alliterative powers rolling in his mind—Cents and sense and silver storm, and only silver keeps you warm.

Eddie, of course, could not be told of this, could not be advised of this impact, could not even be warned. It would not be fair of me, not fair to him at all. They think that we cannot think, that we cannot mine the mind, the they of his thought suddenly having the faces of just about everybody he knew in the whole town, in the whole world for all that matter; the finger pointers, the scorners, the nose-in-air judges, the temperate pretenders, the closet drunks, a vile collection of hoax and hokum spreading all across his wet life. They can't even believe the song that wine sets free or the words that leave off from where they themselves left them, in their darkness, in their lightness, in their great states of privilege. He could feel his face screwing up for a scowl, or a sneer of disdain. "Damn 'em all", he caught himself saying, as if it was a mark of punctuation.

Dusk had long gone over the rim of the hill when they arrived at the dig, as Tony sometimes called it, an angling and huge hole down through rock and gravel and ten million years of tossed stone, a hole whose walls carried the mark of more than one glacier it would probably prove out, a hole thirty-five years in the making, a dream in the minds and at the hands of a man and his son. From the rock walls to the span of the hole to the sense of depth that rose out of the bottom came a fistful of reality. It punched Tony right in the face, made him catch his breath. Thirty-five years at this was more than reality. It had to be more!

He and Eddie had carried lanterns to the site, and a supply of kerosene. They had brought no tools, depending on finding them at the site. The Haskells had, through the long years, etched a path up the long climb of Vinegar Hill, making the ascent much easier than imagined. Tony was not disappointed to find shovels and picks and buckets and ropes in a small shed situated down in the hole, behind a locked chain link fence in front of the shed. The key, without difficulty, was found on a nail behind a pole, and they entered the site. The crest of hell, it seemed to Tony, had risen in their faces; real, with measurement and handles for touching, grasping. If this was daily fare for the Haskells, then the thirty-five years could only be assumed. No one could face this without reacting. Heat, he was sure, rose in their faces, a massive cloud of it that should have been dog=down and cool.

Freddie Rippon's old mushroom house at the edge of the pond, from years past, leaped into his intelligence, how the steam at planting time rose upward like an energy on the loose, the spawn smell as thick in it as tadpoles in a May pool, the taste of sterilized loam still moving on the air from that long-past summer when he and the others had lugged it in baskets to cover the months-treated manure base in the multiple level beds. Back came the manure pile, too; in the dead of winter, stripped to the waist, they had tossed it into the turning machine, spraying it, the fertilizer having its way, steam rising around their bodies from the turning pile as if they were caught in flameless fire. There was, he vaguely remembered, a kind of hell in that, too.

He tried to recall how one whole crop had suddenly gone to disease in one weekend, tried to remember at whose feet that fault could be placed. It all faded too fast as if discovery was truly afoot. He grasped his smooth-handled, long-handled shovel. He knew where he was. For the time being anyway.

Under the glare of the lanterns, they dug and picked their way through shale and stone for more than two hours, talking and grunting and drinking their way to wherever it was going to take them; China or hell, it getting sweeter by the minute, until Eddie lay down his shovel and placed himself beside it, his second day within a day of labor suddenly over and done with.

"My ass is dragging, Tony, and I feel like I'm some damn kind of idiot for being here, never mind breaking my ass at the same time. I'm tired and now I feel like I don't give a hoot if we never find our way home again. I just want to sleep a while, but you can have the dreams. Just let me be." Vapor came with his words, a wet mixture of muscatel and syntax. His lower lip had begun to drag itself under his words; the B's and P's and V's falling away first, the first casualties of speech, shot down in mid-sentence.

Eyes he no longer trusted had long since called for something at the back of his brain, and he seemed to meld himself into the floor of the hole, his back twisting about until it found its mating with Earth. When his eyes closed, his breath coming a hoarse escape, now and then a bubble at the corner of his mouth, Tony knew his friend could probably sleep the night away, if need be.

The shovel in Tony's hands was an instrument indeed, and it pried under the pressure of his foot at the floor of the hole, tipped at the right touch and the right angle and came up with a mouthful of basic earth. Home was where he was, in his own place and the dream beating at him as real as the stones about him. With apparent ease, he tossed the shovelful to the next level above his shoulders. Across the span of his back nothing fought back for another hour. He could shovel with all the John Deeres and all the Napoleon Demarses of the world, legends of their own, that was for sure. For long hours he could shovel, and in the worst weather and under the eyes of the hardest boss imaginable, and fighting the spill of Mother Earth all the time, all the way. They rarely thought about Mother Earth fighting back, but he knew.

The shovel rang at the touching, as it hit at stones in the pile, as it came back down to where his feet were, as it flashed in the light of the lantern like some sword being wielded in the half light of history.

He was glad his friend was asleep, that he was, for all intents and purposes, alone at this task, that the silence between strokes and slices and swings up over his head was meant for his ears alone. It didn't matter what he'd find, not on this night or any one night, but that it was waiting there for him, as cold and as clear and as bright in its shining as any treasure would be, a perfect end of any dream; the eyes closed, the shine still coming unstuffed from the long years of burial, the spill of all the years at his very feet. That was the way it would be. It didn't have to be this night. He knew that. It didn't have to be now, not at this precise time. Perhaps it didn't have to be in this hole.

He smiled at the buzzing all about him, the two lamps whirring away like slight engines, now and then small delicate wings coming past him in the air, the light itself throwing a shine up on the walls and leaping straight upwards out of the hole.

Only some distant star can see this light, he thought, the shaft of it climbing outward on its own beacon, its own endless journey, pursuing the star. To address a star, like this, was part of the dream, part of the treasure itself. This was proof positive! Now it had hands and knuckles to it, stiff forearms able and adept and sufficient for the job. Eddie could never know it, and was better asleep; this was the part that Eddie would never be able to handle, this coming so close, this spanning such distances to come so close.

An awesome energy traversed his shoulders and his upper arms. None of the past day was lingering there in the muscles. He felt the handle of the shovel, knew its smooth surface much like his own skin, could even feel the sense of his own sweat down inside it, the way sap lays under bark and skin of trees. God, he felt strong and close to something. Perhaps that star might at this moment be closer than it would ever be.

The dull thud at the tip of the shovel had talked to him, not only through his ears, but totally. Into his hands and up the stiffness of his arms it came, through the quick riot of nerves suddenly on red alert, through all the passageways of recognition. It was wood! At its tip was wood, a cavernous wood, a chesty wood, an enclosing wood. Promise poised itself, like awards' night and names to be named. Light leaped at his back, behind his head. Down through the awesome sky of darkness he could feel the star draining, down through the thirty-five years of a hole. For a moment everything was frozen and he'd know this time forever; not a single moth traversed the light's span, not a sound was made or heard; above him, millions of miles away but at his back, the weight of a star was known. He did not look at his friend, sure that Eddie would not wake up no matter what he did. This was his time.

He scraped slowly with the shovel blade, moving gravel and hardpan and small rocks across a flat surface.

The star, though, was heavy. It bore down on him, but the tool was like a toothpick in his hands. John Deere and Napoleon DeMars be damned. They'd not known this, the light of such a star warm on the back of the neck, and dry was his throat, and dry his lips. He dared not seek the wine bottle someplace behind him. In this vacuum, he heard nothing. Even the silence was heavy, field of an anode, grip of a battery, the moon held at bay from good old Mother Earth.

Cleared, the wooden surface he'd hit was about two feet by three feet. That it was man-made seemed obvious. In the air hung his father's face, his father's words about dreaming the good life. The sweetness of the wine came back like a retort. It crawled in his mouth smoothly crusty as talc or chalk. It coated his teeth, more so the backside nearer his tongue. At investigation it had granules as small as anything the tongue tip could isolate. The star loomed. He wasn't sure now whether it was overhead or underfoot, but that it was here!

Now a muscle began to talk to him, high on his back, just under one shoulder, at first an ache as dull as a starting toothache not yet localized, then telling of its small rawness. Perhaps it was descendent, alighting from someplace far away. Eddie could never understand all of this. It would drive him off the hill in a mad hurry. It would drive him off, noisily on his way. He'd fall, he'd scramble, he'd tear his knees. There'd be a glut of curses and terror in his heart, for this is where it had all been coming, all the damn time, all the crazy time, all the days and all the nights and all the bottles and all the kegs and all the nips secreted in pockets from bosses and supervisors and the merest of friends when his throat had been driest. He'd been coming here since his father had told him of the good life that dreams would bring him to. No longer were there any secrets. It was all out here in the open in this magnificent pit under the weight of a single star; and then he could hold off no longer, and the bottle came alive in his hand and leaped upward and emptied downward and celebration came his due with the sweet mustiness working its reverent way.

The star was still heaviest on his head, the whole onus of it; not on his shoulders or his back, for he could have shoveled forever, but on his head, thick with a headache and a throb and the punch of a single star no man had ever known.

Struggling for leverage, he finally managed the tip of the shovel under one long edge of the flat surface at his feet. Like a crow bar, the long-handled shovel exerted enough energy to pry loose a piece of wood. Gold and silver and stones shone up at him! His father's face, old bottles, old inscriptions, odd shining, the loosing of dreams, the whole angular mass of lights and reflections, all came at once, blinding him, a blitz of a blitz of light and color he'd never know again.

It was the barest and most lucid moment of his life that came at him then. And he knew he'd be trapped. That life would change so dramatically and so abysmally he could never catch up to where he was right now.

All of it he saw, and there were no dreams and no silence and no small darkness where he could huddle himself alone with his memories.

Dreamer Tony Falcone, the star burning on his neck, still a ponderous weight in his mind, tipped the bottle once more to his lips, and drank off the contents. Then slowly he began to cover the star buried so long at his feet.

Stars, too, are constantly ranked, even when they're caught in the act.

The Boy with a Crooked Mouth

It was never what he said, The Boy with a Crooked Mouth, but how he said it, the way he sneered and looked down at people, at people who did menial tasks. He looked down at maids, truck drivers, sheep ranchers and even firemen when there was no fire. He had little use for landscapers and log splitters, men who froze ice cream, men who climbed poles to put up wires or women who spent long hours making clothes for other people.

Whatever he said, the mean way he said it, the way the words came out of his mouth, made his mouth crooked. The words came with something almost visible hanging on them, pulling at his mouth, like spidery webs or tree moss or ghostly strings of a sort. And his mouth always got twisted and screwed up and made him look odd. He never once realized it. Nobody ever told him, "Go look in a mirror at the way your mouth looks whenever you talk." Nobody ever said to him, "Go talk to the mirror and tell us what you see."

They let him go on talking because his father was the richest man in the town. This was the town where the rich man lived on the top of the hill in the biggest house. It was the house, as The Boy with a Crooked Mouth would say, closest to the stars. "Some nights, if you don't know, I can almost reach out and touch my stars."

Words like those words really stretched his mouth out of shape and made him look so silly and so plastic that people did not laugh, they pitied him so much. "My stars!" they would say to themselves. "My stars!" sounding like, "My word!" and small glee filled their eyes. The Boy with a Crooked Mouth particularly liked Orion, sitting up there on top of everybody in the whole universe. Orion, he thought, must be much like his own father, princely, top of the mark, one of a kind. And, he often said to himself, the kind of a man I will become someday.

One day a new boy came into town. He was tall and had red hair. His bright eyes and handsome face put him in the limelight right away. While he walked about the town that was new to him, he whistled. Every place he went he whistled and people knew he was coming, or knew he was going. All kinds of whistle sounds came from his lips; long whistles and short snappy whistles and train whistles and bird whistles and bird songs, and even ship whistles sounding as if they were far at sea. When he did a whole song while whistling, people would marvel at his range of notes and how beautiful the tones were.

When The Boy with a Crooked Mouth tired of all the attention being paid to The Boy Who Whistled All the Time, he walked up to him and said, "I bet you think you're pretty special the way you can whistle. I don't think you can whistle that good." He turned and pointed off to the house on the top of the hill. "I live up there. Where do you live? What does your father do for work? Does he work in the fields? Is your mother a maid? If she needs a job, I might be able to get her one."

His mouth was as crooked as it ever had been. It was like a scar that had healed from a bad wound, or a bolt of lightning caught in its place in a dark sky. Jagged it was, and wretched. It made his eyes look funny and out of kilter.

The Boy Who Whistled All the Time did not answer the questions. Instead, looking right at the other boy, said, "Why is your mouth so crooked? Did you get hurt? Have you fallen on your head? Are you angry at me because you cannot whistle?" He stopped for a moment and looked closely at the boy's crooked mouth. "I doubt that you could ever whistle, your mouth is so crooked, so out of shape. It's as if it's bent or broken. I probably couldn't teach you how to whistle no matter how hard I tried."

"I can do anything you can do." Nobody had ever talked to him like this. It was strange. He wondered if he should look in a mirror, but he couldn't make himself do it. His mouth felt perfectly all right to him.

"Not with that crooked mouth," the new boy said. "You couldn't begin to whistle with a mouth like that in a hundred years." Off he walked, a glorious tune rising from his lips, a song that made people stop in their tracks, listen to the song, and remember the words that went with the music. A lot of them thought about olden times when they were young. All along the way, people waved at him and raised their arms happily over their heads.

And The Boy with a Crooked Mouth saw it and wondered again about the mirror.

That night he talked about it with his father. "It'll come to you some day, my son," the father said. "You'll be able to whistle and you'll be happy for a while, but then, when it doesn't bring you any money or won't get groceries for you or pay bills, you might want to try something else." He smiled, patted his son on the head and said, "Like working in the bank when the right time comes."

"But what about this new boy? He keeps on whistling and he seems so happy and so are those who hear him. He doesn't have to pay any bills."

"Listen, my son," his father said, "Whatever you do in this life, just make sure people look up to you. Not down on you. That's what's important. Where you fit in this world."

"Like always living on top of the hill in the biggest house?" the boy said. Neither he nor his father saw how crooked his mouth had become once again.

One day the old gardener, who worked on top of the hill at the biggest house, carved a whistle out of an old piece of wood he had found. When he blew on it a beautiful sound came from it. He cut a few more holes and soon a host of lovely notes leaped into the air.

The Boy with a Crooked Mouth heard the notes and came running around the corner of the big house. The old gardener, whose name was

Renee Persimmon, had always smiled at the little man of the big house. He had always been kind, and the boy knew it. Renee was one person he had no disrespect for, and did not look down on him.

"Where did you get such a beautiful whistle, Renee?" he said, and he sat beside the old man on a small bench.

"I made it from an old piece of wood. It was a pretty piece of wood, though. It had such a nice grain to it, long and smooth like a canoe or kayak or a swimmer in the water. I decided not to burn it and not to throw it away because most all things have some kind of use, are worthy in themselves."

"All things?" The Boy with a Crooked Mouth said. He listened to more beautiful notes coming from the whistle. "All things? Are you sure?" He did not know softness had begun at the corners of his lips. The music was still beautiful and Renee nodded his agreement. The boy said, "Will you teach me, Renee. I would love to be able to play that whistle the way you do."

"Why would you want that, Armand?" Renee said, deciding it was time to call the boy by his given name.

The Boy Who Once Had a Crooked Mouth said, "I think it would make people happy. It makes me happy. The Boy Who Whistles All the Time makes people happy." His lips were really soft now, and his mouth was no longer screwed up like a bolt of lightning or an ugly old scar. "Perhaps it would make my father smile to hear me play that whistle."

Renee Persimmon, the old gardener, said, "I don't think you need any lessons, Armand. You look like you can play it right off the bat. Here, try it," and he handed him the whistle and saw how soft and pleasant the boy's mouth was and how music would soon have its rightful place with him.

"Wait until The Boy Who Whistles All the Time hears this," he said as he played some beautiful notes. "It might be the beginning of a beautiful friendship."

"Yes," Renee Persimmon said, "an old friend of mine said that once in a movie a long time ago."

A spilt lip sometimes makes a recovery, if the punctuation is correct.

I Am What I Am Not

Sometimes, a puzzle just has to be disentangled.

The voice, deep at times, sometimes a tone lighter, and usually female in its tenor, came out of the near darkness every night to Hobart "Hobie" Spurt, octogenarian, reader of clouds, fog banks, permanent tree disappearance, erosion, mysteries abounding in all of life. All the voice said was, "I am what I am not."

Hobie would sit on his porch or at his window looking down on the high tide of the river where it came to the foot of the First Iron Works in America, and in reflections cast off from the mirror surface see the dark images of the ancient Scottish indentured laborers at their work. They could run wheelbarrows of bog matter and iron ore with the best of the brickie laborers he had worked with in his youth. Sometimes he saw the flighty spirits and shadows of young boys, long-lost friends, who drowned while riding the winter-time buckeys or ice floes on the Saugus River. Once he saw a man trying to push with difficulty a piano down an embankment into the river. He thought nothing of it and weeks later heard that the man had been missing for weeks. He never thought of it until the night the voice came again.

The sadness grazed him, at times invaded him. But when each of them was accompanied by the mysterious voice, the voice out of darkness, the figures seemed to come alive for him.

And the words were always the same; "I am what I am not." Never different, "I am what I am not." No change in the enunciation, he believed.

"I am what I am not."

In the morning, at the side of the porch where the voice seemed to issue from, he found an old twisted piece of rope perhaps the neighbor's dog had brought in, the dog always gnawing at something, like a pup working its teeth into shape. The dog had been busy, it appeared, because it was not the first time that such a gnarled piece of hemp was found on his property and was obviously from some mooring down at the river, a line rotted or broken loose by strain or chewed away from its task.

The night he saw one of the lost boys whip off his jacket and holding one sleeve of it, tried to toss the other end to his friend who had slipped off the buckey into the water, he saw their faces as clearly as if they were on the other side of the window, looking in at him. And the voice was there, with them, beyond the glass, somewhat muted, but enunciated clearly: "I am what I am not." Both of the boys were lost and the voice fell silent for the time being; *enough pain for one night*, it might have said, though Hobie could not believe that possibility.

Again, that night he prayed for them, hoping it was the illusion of a haunting from the witching hour at the end of a bad day, the distaff side of a nightmare. And nothing more.

But the voice from darkness said, with repeated fervor, "I am what I am not." Different words were stressed at different hearings, with his attempts to pin down what was really being stressed.

Yet he also realized that he'd never been hurt in all of these scenes, these offerings "from the other side." had never been threatened by this … this … Whatever.

There were evenings that Hobie dared not go to bed, fearing he would miss an episode where a lost person was found, came back, was whole again. One of those evenings, he saw one of the Scottish serfs slam another laborer over the head with a shovel. It was not boys playing around on the edge of darkness.

It was real stuff, but perhaps only real in the mind.

And where else, mind you, can it be? he wondered, the tone in his voice, the intent, the outcome, giving him a small touch of humor. But it was hardly worth a laugh, though he did manage a small one.

And with that scene came a scene with Hobie in it, drawing the mysteries into such a relationship that seemed to drag him into a significant enlightenment. He was 20 at this sudden reoccurrence, digging in a trench of the reconstruction of the Iron Works on its way to becoming a National Historic site, when his shovel unearthed a human skull, the skull with a break in it where one ear had been. Yet, in spite of the true sight down in the trench, he swore someone spoke. "At last," a voice said, as if someone had been waiting for Hobie. Though he tried, Hobie could not fend off those words.

The archeologist of the site said, in an offhand way, "Sure looks old. Sure looks like an accident happened to the old buck and he somehow got buried where he fell. See that dirt about him, that's clear sand, that's almost untouched, virgin soil. He must have been digging here and died here and the wall of the trench must have fallen in on him."

More pith than pity in those words, Hobie thought.

Oh, a soul cast adrift without a simple prayer.

For over 60 years the discovery of the skull and other bones had bothered Hobie, until the night, right from his porch, he saw that skull get hit with the blade of a shovel. Of course, it was 60 years too late to say anything.

The night of his 84th birthday, warm for late winter, the voice called him again, the call the same as ever, the words the same as ever, only the mere tone of them with an edge of difference; "I am what I am not."

It was well past midnight for him and for his due sleep when the words came. He felt bad, as had happened before in recent incidents, and put on his slippers and went outside. The high tide in the river was catching lights from the police and fire station, red lights from traffic control bouncing off the river's smooth surface. Eternity itself sat in the widening sky without measurement except for the river disappearing behind the slim shadow of Round Hill and the sky disappearing behind Vinegar Hill, Indian remnants in one place, pirate gold and jewels in the other, each with revelations yet to come.

"I am what I am not," said the shadows, said the voice, now husky. A forgotten movie actress made a face for the voice, dark hair hanging in a lovely mass, one eyebrow arched, her lips pursed for kiss or curse, he was not sure. Then he stepped once more on a twisted piece of rope.

"Dog's at it again," he said. "Klem's been down to the river, at the moorings." The vision of the black and white spaniel came up behind his eyes. "I've got to get down there someday and see how many boats have floated off because that damned dog's been chewing on their lines." He smiled as he imagined a few dories, lobstermen's dories, loose on the river, the tide going out, and the dories on errant rides, the hardy lobstermen waving and yelling frantically on the pier as if each loose dory had a passenger aboard.

Hobie kicked the rope off the patio and onto the driveway pavement.

"I am what I am not," said the voice again, as if he had kicked someone in the rear end.

Then, as if to change his train of thought, night overpowered him with its beauty; stars, like shooting galleries, had unloaded all their ammunition up into it, or like golf balls sparkling on the local driving range and the recovery vehicle was out of order. He laughed again at his images, thought about the numbers of ropes that had appeared beside his house, thought about the voice coming at him so clearly that it was more than a message.

It was, he thought, a statement from a deity, a godhead, some being from beyond his understanding, beyond his experience, beyond any bounds of logic, but saying something that counted. A command? A plea? A bare statement?

"Perhaps," he said, the humor still finding its way in him, "it's a witch." He added a stern pronouncement as he carried himself slowly up the stairs to his bedroom, "Aha, I am caught up in witchery. I wonder if it's a good witch or a bad witch, like the good witches of Oz, Glinda and Gayellete of North and South or the bad witches, Nessarose and Elphaba of East and West."

There was a difference, known or unknown, in all of them. And that made him say, aloud as he plied his way one step at a time, "It might have been in her tone, or the way she stressed one word ahead of another one time and then stressed another word in a later message, but each message coming with the same words."

Slippers off, about to go to bed, some sudden clarity of his questions came rising as if it had followed him up the stairs to his room.

It made him yell.

"There is a difference!" he exclaimed. "There is a difference. I've found it! I've found it!" His mind had leaped up from a soggy mass to find the bright light and he went back down the stairs.

In the driveway he picked up the clutter of rope he had kicked aside. He grabbed it in one hand, unrolled the twist in it and the voice said, so that he understood it perfectly, "I am what I am, Knot."

A shift came, a surge in his hand, and a most beautiful maiden formed before him, the maiden he had dreamed of all his life, and she kissed the old man on the lips and said, "Knot thanks you for her freedom, for untying her, and will remember you all her time."

And she was gone into another world.

The Boy with the Golden Ring

The boy's name was John. He was twelve-years old and a street person. You could tell by the clothes he wore. They were old and worn and torn, and dirty looking. One pocket of his thin jacket was missing, his pants were short, his socks did not match, and he had no hat on his head. His hair was very dark and he was standing in front of the Sligo Bakery near the big cathedral. A tall man in worn clothes was standing with him, and they were looking at food in the bakery window. Around them swirled the cold wind and the snow of a storm on a late December evening.

The baker Connaughton looked out the window at them. A strange glow was fuzzy around the boy's head. Connaughton was drawn to him. He had been pulled from the back of the bakery when he saw the boy standing at the window looking so hungry. In Connaughton's blood raced a new sensation. He could feel it coursing. It was the same feeling he had when the anthem was played. When he heard a beautiful psalm it came to him, or when a far and lovely voice at nightfall sang an old song he had nearly forgotten, the special way it came out of the past bringing all kinds of delightful company with it, like a Percy French song echoing from the Cliffs of Mohr. Oh, he thought, the deliriums of joy.

Connaughton waved them into the shop, in from the cold and the swirling snow. The tall man shook his head and pointed to the boy. Even in his shabby clothes, the man bore to Connaughton a sense of regality and pride, yet he had a kindly presence about him. The man refused a second invitation and again pointed to the boy. As bidden, the boy entered the bakery and Connaughton put six rolls and a cup of coffee in a bag. The boy looked back at the man standing outside the window.

"My father says you are a good man," the boy said to Connaughton, "but he's not hungry right now." The baker and the boy turned and the man was gone. The boy ran outside and the man was gone. The snow was worsening and it was colder. The boy cried, "My father has left me. My father has gone." He looked at Connaughton and said again, in the saddest voice Connaughton had ever heard, "My father has left me."

Connaughton did not know what to do. His job he could not leave, and there was no place to take the boy. Then he saw a street person he recognized, a good man by the name of Samuel Haggard. He called him over to the bakery.

"Samuel," he said, "this boy's name is John and his father has left him. I'm afraid of what will happen to him in the night. Can you take care of him?"

Samuel looked at the boy John and saw the golden light that was like a faint glow around the boy's head. When he put his hand on the boy's shoulder, he was warmed by the touch. "I know a place where he can sleep," he said. It's only a closet, but there's lots of paper and cardboard and he will not freeze."

Connaughton gave them more rolls and coffee and went back to work. Only when he was inside did he realize that he had not been cold at all when he had gone outside in the bitter night to talk to Samuel. He waved at the boy John and Samuel as they walked off into the darkness.

As they walked, Samuel said he was sorry that the boy's father was gone.

The boy John said, "Do not feel sorry for me, Samuel. My father loves me. Some time he will come back for me." The golden glow was stronger around the boy's head.

Other street people that knew Samuel came up to him as they walked. "Who is this boy, Samuel?" they said. They stared at the boy

John. Many street people stared and asked the same question. Many of them had seen the glow around the boy's head, though some had not seen it. They did not know what to make of their old friend Samuel and the strange new boy who looked so much like they did. His clothes were like their clothes. He looked as lonely as they looked. He had no real place of his own to go to on a cold December night, no real place to put down his head for the night; no fire, no blanket, no cradling arms.

Samuel said to the boy John, "Would you like to go to the cathedral to warm up before we go to a place to sleep?"

The boy John said, "Don't you go to the cathedral to pray, Samuel?" The glow was more golden and brighter and made Samuel uneasy, not sure of what it was. He just knew that here was something different around the boy and around his own person.

In the cathedral, a crowd of street people had gathered. Word had spread quickly in the alleys and the lanes and the byways about the boy with a golden ring about his head. Most of the people agreed it was a ring. Not one of them had called it a halo.

In the subway stations, also, people spoke about him. Word spread up and down the Green Line and the Red Line and the Orange Line. On the back sides of chimneys, and tight against warm walls, and on warm exhaust grates, the street people talked about the boy. There was a buzz and a hum about him. The word carried far and wide. It rippled and ran with the wind.

The people who came to the cathedral at first were seedy looking. Their clothes were in tatters. Some of them wore rolls of cloth around their feet and about their waists. Some wore old sneakers or thin worn shoes. Few of them had good jackets or coats or scarves or warm gloves for their tortured hands. They came to look at the boy with a golden ring about his head and who had no place to go to call his own, the boy who was so much like them.

The next night Samuel took the boy John back to the cathedral. Now hundreds of people were there. Some of them laughed and scoffed and said they could not see any light at all, never mind a golden ring. Many new arrivals wore nice clothes and heavy coats and thickly padded jackets against the cold. High boots many of them wore and scarves and great warm gloves on their hands. Indeed, some of them did not laugh for they believed they saw the golden light.

Samuel brought the boy John back to the cathedral each night. It was getting close to Christmas and the crowds grew and the bishop called for police help with the crowds along the cluttered streets. All kinds of people from all over were coming to the cathedral to see the boy. You could tell by the clothes they wore, or what kind of vehicle brought them to the great church.

Samuel warmed up in the cathedral each time and the boy John prayed for his father to come back. He kept telling Samuel that his father loved him and would come back for him. Samuel did not know what to believe. He just knew he had to bring the boy back each night in spite of the crowd's gawking at him. The snickers and the scoffing bothered Samuel. At times he grew impatient with people he had known for a long time.

"He's just a boy whose father left him," explained Samuel as often as he could. But he did not believe what he was saying. The light was getting too bright for him to handle. He asked a friend to bring the boy John to the cathedral the next night. It would be Christmas Eve.

All day the snow fell. The temperature also fell with the late hours. The darker it got, the colder it got.

But a greater crowd than ever before came on Christmas Eve. They packed the old cathedral. Every seat was taken. The aisles were full. People stood all around looking at the boy John down in the front row. Some saw the light. Some did not. But none of them left the cathedral then. Some were afraid to go. Some, indeed, were afraid to stay.

The bishop, at the back of the altar, tried desperately to see the golden glow. He was not sure what he was seeing. A young priest,from a nearly forgotten order, saw the golden ring around the boy's head. Clearly, he saw it. He spoke to the bishop for a few minutes and came to the front of the congregation.

"We know why some of us have come here tonight. Some have come for the right reason. Some have not. It may be that some will be rewarded and some will not. And that may be as it was meant to be. I will ask the boy John to come up here and talk to us if he feels like it."

He extended his open hand to the boy John.

The boy John went to the front of the altar. "I am very nervous," he said."

"Do not be nervous," the young priest replied. "We are all sorry that your father has left you."

"Do not be sorry for me. I love my father very much," the boy John said, "and he loves me. Some time he will come back to get me."

"Do you want to tell us anything?" the young priest said. He looked directly at the boy John and did not look at the bishop at the back of the altar.

"One night, at a campfire on a cold night, my father took off his coat and gave it to a man who did not have a coat. He said, 'Now we will both be warm.'"

The young priest did not say anything. The bishop did not say anything. The boy John looked at the huge gathering. No one in the congregation said anything. No one did anything. The huge cathedral was silent, silent in the nave, silent in the apse, and silent in the transept. You could not hear people breathe or cough or blow their noses as you did at other times. Their feet also were still and silent on the floor. The boy John, with the golden glow around his head, said, "That's the beautiful picture I have. It's the most beautiful picture of all. That each person who has a coat or a heavy jacket would give it to a person who does not have a warm coat or a heavy jacket. Or give a warm hat to someone who has no hat or a scarf to someone who has no scarf or a great pair of gloves to someone whose hands might freeze before this night is over. My father says you will be warmer, and my father loves me very much, and I love my father even though he has gone from me for this while."

Again, for long minutes, there was silence in the great cathedral. Nothing moved. No one moved. Stillness was sharp as the cold. It was only the wind that was heard, from the belfry and at the windows as if it were trying to get inside.

The boy John looked at the congregation. Now, as if predicted, more people began to see the glow that they had not seen before. Inside them things were working they had no control over. Then, in the midst of the great silence, one man in the fifth row, in a fine and heavy coat, thick and furry, stood up and took the coat off his shoulders and handed it to a man sitting in front of him. That man had no coat but wore a thin and worn sweater atop another thin and worn sweater. No words were exchanged.

Then another man stood in the silence and gave his coat. And another. And another. And a pair of great fleece-lined gloves moved from one pair of hands to another, and a scarf, and more and more, until the sounds of giving swelled throughout the whole insides of the cathedral as if a soft wind was blowing.

And the boy John smiled at all the people and at the young priest and at the bishop. Then he said, loud enough for everybody in the cathedral to hear, "I do not want anyone who gave his coat or hat or gloves to another person to get cold tonight going home. If there is a taxicab driver who can help get those people home, everyone will be warmer."

In the back row a man stood up and said, "I have my cab and I'll call my friends who have cabs."

When the people left the cathedral a short time later, there were many cabs in the street, their lights glowing golden through the edge of darkness. It looked like a parade of taxicabs.

And Samuel Haggard, coming late to the cathedral, saw in the distance, in the swirling snow, in the region past the crowd, the boy John walking off into the endless night with his hand in his father's hand.

And the glow over his head had faded away.

Some have known that moonlight is often as powerful as sunlight, though it's the little brother (or sister).

Swan River Daisy

Chester McNaughton Connaughton, aptly named for both sides of the family, landowner in the new world, squeezer of pennies and nickels at the very corpulence of coin, embarrassed at times by his own good fortune where his roots had once been controlled and ordained by potatoes and turnips or the lack thereof, gazed over the latest acquisition of a two-acre parcel abutting his prime abode and wondered how he could best utilize it. Mere coinage, he had early assessed, would apply the jimmy bar under Carlton Smithers and separate him from the land in their town of Saxon, not far from Boston. Carlton was old, alone, susceptible. It would be a piece of cake. It was, subsequently and as he had forecast, a swift steal, and papers and proper process moved the property under the shield of his name.

A big man in his own right, massive across the shoulders, Chester, even as a dreamer of large proportions, was given to talking to his father long gone down the pike, from a runaway case of pneumonia, to better pasture. The old gent had once called it *"a greater kingdom and a lesser court."* Still civil in such matters, Chester addressed his father as "sir," never once forgetting his manner of address.

"Sir," he said this day, "how can I best use this land? The farmer is no longer in me; no endless hours, no thievery of land and what it will allow to be taken from it, I do not envision. What would you propose? I would by design do whatever you suggest." On his porch, the sun wavering its heat across the width of the two acres, Chester transposed himself into his study mode.

Now it takes all kinds of beliefs to manage oneself in this world, and commerce or business demands certain of those beliefs come into the fate of a man. Chester heard his father say, in the same enigmatic voice, the same wonder of voice, the simple words, *"Swan River Daisy,"* the words a barely audible breath coming upon his porch, like an aside from forever. The long-gone old man had not entirely eluded him. A sense of trust redoubled itself in him as he heard the echo say again, from some parallax athwart the universe, *"Swan River Daisy,"* and repeating, *"Swan River Daisy."*

Acceptance struck him. Oh, he knew that sun-yellow flower well, a hardy, deep-root grower that dispelled an easy pull of root work in the fall. One year a decade or so earlier, he had planted the whole flower bed across the front of the old colonial house with the tenacious daisies, waiting for their yellow waves to unfold a day in May, a wave a teasing breath of wind could set to dancing, the daisies standing so tall. Both the blossoming and the root work came back to him in swift recall. Did the old man mean to have him construct a greenhouse on the property, to specialize in Swan River Daisies? Was that the evolution of the simple answer a soft wind had brought him across the field? Should he plant the whole field with such golden color it would attract tourists? Should he run horses, like roans and pintos, through the field, and to what end? What good means is such advice without fair and equitable interpretation?

At length, in this quandary, the sun nodded his head and closed his eyes, and the old man said again from off the porch yet at immeasurable distance, *"Swan River Daisy."*

Came upon him eventually turmoil and noise and his daughter crying out to him, "Father! Father! Look, look at the field!"

Upon his new property sat the most gorgeous Mississippi paddle wheel steamboat he had ever seen. It was red and blue of color and proud in its bearing and was smoking at its single black stack. Bales of cotton, like pale brown dominoes, stood on the prow of its deck and the paddle wheel astern of it, like a huge radius, spun itself through slow, angry revolutions. But there were no passengers crowding its deck, no crew evident about its surfaces, no movement other than smoke in a single column drifting upward to dispersion and the paddle wheel only partly visible in its circular passage.

Boldly printed in large yellow letters against the blue hull was the name, "Swan River Daisy."

In less than the passage of one hour he was nearly assaulted by the Building Inspector who had come in answer to neighbors' complaints, his eyes popping, his hands in agitated gesture. "How did you get it here? Did you have a permit? Do you have a permit? Was there a building plan submitted to Town Hall before this traffic? I suspect, sir, that you have violated many laws and regulations and will be held accountable."

Chester shrugged his shoulders. "I did not bring it here. How could I do that? It was just there. My daughter, in great confusion, yelled at me and said, 'Look in the field.' There it was."

"Is that your field?" The inspector was indeed young, indeed officious and surly in manner, the way Chester looked upon him, and wore his hair long and uncombed.

"Yes, I bought it quite recently." A pup is still a pup, Chester announced to himself.

"I suggest, sir, that this must go all the way to the Town Manager and the Board of Selectman. You, most likely, as I have said, have broken all kinds of rules. That plot is not zoned for business." The inspector was young, snotty-nosed, arrogant in an imperial and puerile manner at one and the same time, and was shaking his head and pointing the most possible accusatory finger at landowner Chester McNaughton Connaughton, smarting at the surliness.

"What business is that, inspector?" Chester could not bring himself to call the young man *sir*. That was reserved for his father. His father came from that distant point again, that far parallax, *"Swan River Daisy."*

The wide-eyed young inspector, obviously not in on the other conversation, replied, from his haughty countenance, "Why, that of transportation, having a river boat, delivering cotton bales, obviously a horde of passengers who are below deck and gambling illegally." His head shook in a fearfully authoritative manner, superior counsel judging the Swan River Daisy from his dais, and thus judging Chester McNaughton Connaughton.

"Delivering bales where?" Chester's hands were on his hips, his arms like sails, a big man towering over the young judge in pants though not in robe.

"Why, the next port of call, perhaps." The young man looked down past the fields the way one might look down river. Fluster, for the lack of another expression, came on him.

"I must report this to higher authorities. I will call the electric and telephone and cable companies to see if any of their wires have been cut or disturbed. This is highly unusual. Improper displacement of utilities most certainly has been commissioned in this transport. Think of all your neighbors so unceremoniously impacted. Perhaps half the town. Why haven't I been so informed?"

In the most inquisitive gesture, he cocked his head to one side, a half smile at his mouth, as if to say *you can let me in on this*, and said, "How did you ever in this world navigate the underpass from the main highway? That seems quite impossible."

"I suspect it does look that way, but I did not bring it here. I did not build it. I did not order it. I did not wish for it. And I assure you, I know nothing about the underpass or the overpass or how it was, as you say, navigated." Chester suspected there was in his own eyes a merry twinkle at this point. He consciously depressed the words, "Perhaps there's been a change of tide."

"But, sure as heaven, you are responsible for it." The finger was wagging at Chester once more. "It's on your property, sir, and you are therefore responsible. I hope you have insurance."

"For what?" replied Chester, still hearing the far voice saying, "*Swan River Daisy*."

"For the obvious damages you have incurred getting it here."

"Getting what here?"

"Getting the Swan River Daisy onto your property, that's what. I can read the name on the hull. I know what a Mississippi steamboat is, and a stern paddle wheeler for all that. You can't fool me in these matters. I assure you I have read *The Adventures of Tom Sawyer*. I know about the big river and the boats. I even saw the movie, Tom and Huck and Becky in the cave. And Injun Joe."

A pause came upon the young inspector, jaw hanging slack, then a distant light came into his eyes as he stuttered in saying while pointing at the Swan River Daisy, "This… this, sir... this is not Saxonish. This is," and he held his breath in proper caesura before he nearly shouted out, "Mississippian." As he walked away, Chester McNaughton Connaughton saw a definite slump had accosted the young man's shoulders.

In less than another hour, a parade of men and two women came to Chester McNaughton Connaughton as he and his daughter Chadra were leaning on the fence that girded the new parcel of land, and the Swan River Daisy still puffing a thin line of black smoke, the wheel still turning mysteriously into the earth, and as yet no passengers or crew evident.

Counted in that new audience were the Town Manager, the Town Counsel, the Board of Selectmen including two women members, three men from the Planning Board, an energetic member of the Appeals Board who was rapidly making notations on a pad of paper, and citing the length of the Swan River Daisy by use of a visimeter of a special sort. Every man was dressed in a black suit, white shirt and black tie and Chester, whispering to his daughter, said, "They look like hangmen if you ask me." To which the daughter replied, "Especially the women in those deep-rose dresses, so ghastly."

The Town Manager, bristling, holding forth in front of the small parade, addressed Chester McNaughton Connaughton. "My dear Mr. Connaughton, what is going on here?" With his hands on his hips he was still half the size of Chester, yet he had a round face, almost moonlike above the black tie, and deeply-set eyes continuously at measurement. "This disturbance, this disdain. I was at a wedding reception. It is no mean fete to slip away from a wedding reception. I'll have you know. I might have dishonored a constituent."

Chester reminded himself of the change of tide comment and thought well of it. "Do you seek passage, sir? Do you sail? Indeed, I do not, and do not contemplate doing so."

"Is this your craft?" The Town Manager, whose name was Anton Swirling, said to Chester, and then smiled at the two ladies from the Board of Selectmen. He did not know which one he favored best.

"It is not my craft. It is not my boat. It is not my ship."

"Is this your land?"

"We all know this is my land," Chester offered, leaning back against the split rail fence. "I bought it from Carlton Smithers."

The Town Manager smirked for the ladies once more. "At a ridiculously low price, from what I hear."

"Would you have bought it at that price?" Chester said.

"That's beside the point," the Town Manager said.

"Precisely what I say," Chester came back with. "It's all beside the point. This is not my paddle wheeler."

"If it stays here in your field, you will have to pay taxes." In his affirmation, Anton Swirling was holding the hand of one of the ladies of the Board of Selectmen. He squeezed that hand as a sign of his authority and their potential. "That means property taxes, water fees, sewerage fees, all that apply to a place of business. The Assessors are at this moment coming up with a firm billing." He felt puffed and thorough and mightily superior.

"To what business do you refer?" Chester said.

"The business of commerce, sir. It is most evident that this craft is a business enterprise. My god, man, look at the piles of cotton bales on the prow of that craft."

"Do you suggest that I have a cotton field where such cotton is raised?"

"Where you get it, sir, is your concern. Mine is you pay appropriate fees for this business."

"If I offered you for the taking every bale of cotton, would you take them, for free?"

Chester offered. Chadra Connaughton squeezed her father's hand.

"What in heaven's name would I do with bales of cotton? Where would I take them?"

"Your Building Inspector, whom I note did not return with you, suggested the next port of call, down river somewhere."

"My god, sir, there is no river here."

"That is precisely my argument, Mr. Town Manager. There is no river to properly run a business of boats. There is no next port of call. There is no place to deliver the goods of a business. There is nothing. This town has not supplied any services for such a business. And you wish to tax me on those conditions."

"By god, sir, there is a boat in your field and you will pay taxes on it." His voice was a few octaves up on its normal range. The lady of the held hand squeezed him back. He turned to the assessor still madly scribbling on his pad. "I want the whole business of this land sale scrutinized before this day is out. We will get to the root cause for all actions, mark my words. And once you have ascertained the proper tax billing, please present it to Mr. Connaughton." He squeezed the lady's hand and said, in his best manner, "And with a duplicate copy to me so that I can fully watch and control this situation myself, if I must say so."

The parade of authority of the Town of Saxon walked off behind the Town Manager who strutted like a drum major at the head of a band.

Chadra Connaughton tugged her anxiety at her father's sleeve. "Easy, child," he said, "it will be fine with us. We have done no wrong."

When Town Manager Anton Swirling woke in the morning and looked out his back window, hoping to catch the glint of the early sunrise, The Swan River Daisy, on due course, was now crowding his whole back yard.

A strange river needs not have a two-way route.

Lyle's Word on the Lexicon of Forcible Memory

Lyle Goodbrow (an AKA), an avid reader, filled me in on his way with words from the very beginning of our long friendship in the same high school, the words blasting my mind into fragmentation hanging yet, the mass of them like the all-starred firmament coming back in odd times, due times, times crying for help in solitary hours where new ideas shoot like rockets on the loose, the sky calling down words to be heard, white pad written, typed, computerized; the responsibilities of catching them on the fly belonging right here.

Lyle, as I said, says it's so. He never told me once a lie.

Memories hang on me desperate for sounding, for eyes not mine, for those strangers who succumb to a few words, images, my final say in all of this, words free but costly; how connections arise, surprise, stay afloat, stay aboard. In that same high school, a girl turned away from my hello and walked elegantly off to her lifetime, smiling yet, a raving beauty yet, mother-proud, regal in skirts, the perfect edge of temperament. That same day, before anybody else greeted dawn, I slyly tore open my brother's fragile V-mail letter from war's wild Pacific, its onionskin contents marked by a censor's serious look at life. And just a few moments later I also heard my cousin's faint telephone voice for the last time, from a Port of Embarkation somewhere masqueraded on our East Coast, and I still remember his falsetto tone holding back, saying nothing, saying everything important to us.

Others must have ears like I have. Switched to late cool jazz after hearing Giacomo Puccini at his best in New Jersey, poetry books' Jimmy Smith hears regal trumpets, knows what Auden meant, saying, "In the nightmare of the dark /All the dogs of Europe bark," and rich words that fell from my poetic grandfather's lips like reading from an Old World cairn, "the Red Fergus put down," recognized as my own, and war changing everything we know, heathens tossing stones at the other village.

Words and their images carry my heart locked into Saugus whose streets I walk the way I'll walk another paradise, if there's one like this, if I can earn my way to it, where the river comes palpable touching East Saugus, where one sees old pilings and boats, worn by muscle and time, continue journeys back into earth, where marshes turn suddenly brown, then white, and where friends, old, lost and forlorn, herald every corner I turn, telling me they love what I still have.

At Aveiro, Portugal, by the river's mouth, boats scatter as compass points, small scoops on an interminably huge sea rising to the line of sight where gallant Genovese fell off the known world. They wait oarsmen, hands warm with women, mouths rich with memory and signals, whose sons later come to these small boats topping the Atlantic, anchored by thin rope and night's tidal pull. It's where I stood between commotion and silence, spills of *olla podridas* riding air with ripeness, earthly bath scents, night's wet mountings, saw boats move like sea and earth move against a distant cloud. I have questions about the hammer that drove raw poles of moorings into the sea floor; a mustachioed Latin god, laughing at his work while waving to a woman on the strand, sees her, urged from bed or kitchen, eye him eye to eye. An artist could tell us what's missing is important; before dawn, an oarsman knows old calluses where Atlantic sends messages up through heel and calf, through thigh's thew and spinal matter radiant in miles of nerves, while small boats gathered at Aveiro only speak of loneliness.

I know Lyle hears these echoes, even now. The secret, he told me before he died, was he once sat in the same seat in the narrow English classroom where renowned poet Elizabeth Bishop sat during her freshman year at Saugus High School, the building long gone now, but the records are clear about Elizabeth, who lived in 1928 with an aunt at

20 Sunnyside Avenue before she took away some of Saugus-Lynnfield with her, as revealed in her poem, "Just North of Boston," about Route One where Ship's Haven Restaurant, later called "The Ship," half-buried into a hill mere feet from the gunnels, its aft end once pointing at the main road north-south, is ever gone, that bare piece of land now stretching far away, waiting tenancy. The word is that Elizabeth only composed 100 poems in her lifetime, so hard to believe from this end of town.

Just North of Boston

Elizabeth. Bishop
"Winter twilight: miles of advertising.
- One doesn't know whether to laugh or cry.
Lights chasing each other round and round;
lights running at us screaming letters.
If only we didn't know how to read,
or if they screamed Chinese or Arabic,
would we consider them beautiful?
You say "It's possible."
But look - an 18th-century man-of-war
has run aground: She's struggling there
against the rocks, her lights still lit,

directing rescue operations. No -
it's worse: it's *half* a man-of-war.
Now come the wedding clothes for rent:
six brides are standing in a row,
dresses agleam like glare-ice; next, their grooms,
with ruffled shirt-fronts, pink or blue,
all on a brilliant stage, on stilts.
How can they meet? When will they marry?
Gold! *Gold*. A Burmese temple? Balinese?
An oriental-something roof, with grinning
dragons. Just beyond,
an ice-cream cone *a gratte-ciel*
outlined in glowing yellow, glowing rose
on top - the ice cream-strawberry.
Twelve Hereford steer, three Hereford calves

of sturdy plaster are deployed."
As they say locally, "Elizabeth knew her way around."

(This previously unpublished poem appears in a new edition of Bishop's writing. Edgar Alan Poe & The Juke Box" Uncollected Poems, Drafts, and Fragments, edited by Alice Quinn.)

Prior credits and acknowledgments:

Perpetual Magazine
Clever Magazine
Lotus Reader
Outward Link
Troubadour 21
Perigee
Blue Lake Review
Rope and Wire Magazine
Raphael's Village
Danse Macabre
Larks Fiction Magazine
Fullcaps
Artifact Journal
Epiphany Magazine
Nazar Look
Eskimo Pie
Ocean Magazine
Down in the Dirt
Imitation Fruit
Provo Canyon Review
Riverbabble
Literary Yard
Green Silk Journal
Literally Stories
Tulip Tree
Imitation Fruit
Eastlit
Outlook
Poetic Diversity

Orion's Child
Mythaxis
New Hampshire Pulps Live Free or Die
Succour
Rosebud
Fringe
Faith, Hope & Fiction
Adroit
Perpetual Magazine
The Linnet's Wings
Fiction on the Web

The author, #12, now in is 93rd year, once carried the good word (and a soft curse) as well as the leather, as Earl Dudman runs interference downfield for him and opponent Hercules Harristopolous threatens to separate the word, the curse and the ball from his custody.